Merry Christmas, Montana

Merry Christmas, Montana

A Millers of Marietta Romance

Elsa Winckler

Merry Christmas, Montana
Copyright© 2023 Elsa Winckler
Tule Publishing First Printing, October 2023

The Tule Publishing, Inc.

ALL RIGHTS RESERVED

First Publication by Tule Publishing 2023

Cover design by LLewellen Designs

No part of this book may be used or reproduced in any manner whatsoever without written permission except in the case of brief quotations embodied in critical articles and reviews.

This is a work of fiction. Names, characters, places, and incidents are products of the author's imagination or are used fictitiously. Any resemblance to actual events, locales, organizations, or persons, living or dead, is entirely coincidental.

ISBN: 978-1-961544-26-0

Dedication

For my partner, my lover, the father of our kids, Theo.
Thank you for making it so easy to write about love.

Acknowledgements

Thanks to the fabulous team of women at Tule Publishing for all their support and help, especially to Kelly Hunter who has been the editor for this series. It has been such an honor and pleasure to work with her.

I have enjoyed spending time in Marietta, getting to know the fictional town and its people and am seriously considering moving there soon 😊. Thanks to Tule Publishing for giving me the opportunity to use the setting of this magical town to create stories.

And thank you, dear reader, for picking up this story – I love writing about love.

And as always, thanks to my husband Theo, who waited for me – I can't imagine life without you.

Chapter One

R ILEY O'SULLIVAN HAD her camera ready. She was happy with all the pictures she'd taken so far, but as she'd learned over the years as a fashion photographer, the best photos were often taken in unguarded moments. As she watched through her camera lens, the groom put out a hand and gently touched his bride's face, his obvious adoration for the woman in front of him clear for all to see.

Click-click. Smiling, Riley dropped her arm. This would be the best one, her gut was telling her.

It was a glorious day, the first Saturday in August, the air filled with the crisp promise of fall. As the wedding photographer for her cousin Craig and his bride Annie's wedding, she'd been taking pictures since early this morning—first of the bride and her bridesmaids—she'd had to ask her godmother, Aunt Janice, to help with some of them, seeing she was also a bridesmaid—and later of the groom and his groomsmen.

Her happy place was behind the camera lens—always had been—and taking photographs of the happy couple against the backdrop of orange and brown trees was a profoundly beautiful experience.

Taking wedding photos wasn't her usual gig, but when Craig and Annie had asked if she'd be able to be here for the wedding to take the pictures, she'd changed her plans immediately. For her cousin, she'd walk over hot coals if need be. Craig had always been there for her when she'd needed him. To be able to do this for him and Annie was her small way of thanking him for the way he'd always had her back.

She was tired, but it was a good tired. Capturing happy moments for these two people, who so obviously belonged together, was such a privilege and great fun.

And bonus, being busy had one other big advantage—she didn't have to talk to people. As a textbook introvert, she was energized when she was alone. People drained her, but if she was busy doing what she loved, she was able to ignore the near panicky feeling she got when she was in a crowd.

Back in Portland, she had one friend, Elana. They'd met in second grade and had been friends since then. The two of them had always tried to meet up at least once a month, but since Elana had married her college sweetheart, an editor at a well-known publisher, they hardly saw one another these days. Two were as big a crowd as she could handle.

With her camera still in her hand, she walked toward the table where her godmother, Aunt Janice, was sitting. She was not hard to miss. Dressed from top to toe in bright red, a pair of huge silver earrings dangling from her ears, she made a definite statement. Age was just a number, she would always say.

"Dylan still okay?" Riley asked as she crouched down to lift the long tablecloth covering the table. Her three-year-old son was sleeping peacefully on a small mattress. He was growing up way too fast; next month he'd be four. Pulling the blanket over him, she got up. "Thanks, Aunt Janice. Don't you want to go and dance?"

Aunt Janice smiled. "I am enjoying myself from here. I can't believe Craig and Annie have actually invited Carol Bingley to the wedding. She will now have material to keep her gossiping machine going for months." Her eyes twinkled. "And I see Barry Davis is trying his level best to get you to dance with him. I don't even think he's been invited to the wedding."

Putting her camera down, Riley grimaced. "He's just plain scary. He tells me he's sixty."

Janice snorted. "He's probably eighty, but that doesn't seem to stop him from trying to get a young gal to dance with him tonight." Aunt Alice chuckled.

"I don't want to be rude, but if he grabs my arm one more time, I won't be responsible for what I do. I'm going to get something to eat. What about you?"

"I'm fine. Thanks, sweetie." She motioned toward the dancing bridal couple. "I'm so, so happy for Craig and Annie."

Riley grinned. "Clearly besotted with each other. Sure

you don't want anything?"

"I'm sure. Go get something to eat. You've been on your feet all day."

With another quick look under the table to make sure Dylan was fine, Riley headed toward the table with food. Eating had been the last thing on her mind all day, she'd been so busy.

Fortunately, most people already had their food, so she could leisurely look around and decide on what she wanted.

"You've been busy today," a smooth voice said next to Riley.

Warily, she turned her head. It was Mitch. The *yelling brother* as she'd dubbed him. His older sister, Vivian, had married Riley's brother, Aiden, in May and now Annie, his younger sister, was marrying Riley's cousin, Craig. The few times she'd seen Mitch during the past year, he'd either been yelling or threatening to beat up either her brother or her cousin. In fact, Mitch had actually punched Aiden. Mitch had been furious because Vivian was upset and had been crying.

He probably had good reasons why he'd behaved that way. Normally, she'd study someone's face to try and understood a person's behavior. But for some or other strange reason, she'd never been able to get herself to really take a good look at Mitch Miller's face.

"You about to yell at me?" she asked.

Chuckling, he also took a plate and helped himself to the

food. "No yelling tonight, you have my word. Both my sisters are married. For the moment, at least, I'm doing okay. But both Aiden and Craig should know I have my eye on them."

"I'm sure they're shuddering in their boots knowing that." She didn't even try to hide the sarcasm. Mitch Miller was so not her cup of tea.

"You! Camera Girl!" a voice called from behind Riley.

Groaning, she glanced over her shoulder. Yup, the old guy was drunkenly making his way over to her. Again.

Quickly, she put her plate down and grabbed Mitch's hand. "Come on, dance with me. If Harry or Barry or whatever his name is, grabs me one more time tonight… come on!"

But Mitch didn't move. "Maybe if you ask nicely…"

"Camera Girl!" Barry called loudly; this time he sounded much closer than before.

Gnashing her teeth, she laced her fingers with Mitch's. "Please, damn it."

The next minute, Mitch had taken her hand, and lifting their clutched hands, he spun her away from him before pulling her back into his arms. They were dancing.

"I wanted to dance with you!" Barry wailed from the sides.

Ignoring him, Mitch danced her to the middle of the floor. The first few lines of an old song penetrated her befuddled mind. *Something stupid*—one of her mother's favorites.

To her surprise, Mitch was a good dancer. He was barely touching her, but she instinctively knew what his next move was going to be. From the very first step, her body was in perfect sync with his. In silence, they glided over the floor as one.

Dropping his hand from her shoulder, he spun her out. With the corners of his mouth turning up ever so slightly, he pulled her back toward him. As she stepped back into his arms, his hand touched her shoulder before it slipped down her back until warm fingers were touching her bare skin.

Rattled, she inhaled slowly. A mistake. His male scent of… what was it? Vanilla? Suede? Whatever it was found its way into her bloodstream, heating her blood within minutes. What was happening?

Swallowing a groan, she tried to focus on the music, but the words of the lyrics weren't helping. Seriously, she didn't have time for this.

Up until now, she'd had a lovely day. If it hadn't been for the old guy bothering her, she wouldn't be dancing with Mitch, wouldn't have become so aware of his scent, his broad shoulders, his muscled body.

Mitch's hand slid a little farther down her back, and her heartbeat kicked into the next gear as her dopamine levels went ballistic.

And she'd thought dancing with Mitch would be an escape—what had she been thinking?

THE SUBTLE SCENT of orange blossoms floated around Mitch, threatening to overwhelm his already overstimulated senses. *Talk. Say something, anything,* before he did something really stupid. Dancing with the enigmatic Riley was turning out to be more than he'd bargained for.

"So, why don't you want to dance with Barry?" was the first thing that came to mind.

Riley lifted those long lashes, and clear blue eyes looked at him, really looked at him for the first time.

The next lines of the song sank in. Could it be he'd nearly been in the brink of saying something totally stupid? Since the first day he'd laid eyes on the redhead in his arms, she'd literally taken his breath away. She was usually dressed in soft, flowing clothes, big hoops dangling from her ears. With eyes the color reminiscent of fields of lavender, long, red tresses falling down her back, legs that seemed to go on forever, she was breathtakingly beautiful.

However, she'd been such a thorn in his hide during the times she'd been visiting her brother and cousin, he'd tried his best to ignore her. Granted, he'd behaved badly, but he'd been looking out for his sisters, damn it; she didn't have to make fun of his concern and call him the *yelling brother*.

Over the last few days, he'd been busy moving into his new home and hadn't seen Riley before yesterday at the rehearsal dinner. She'd sat at the opposite side of the long table, though, and they hadn't spoken a word.

Tonight, she looked incredible. The bodice of the blush-pink dress she was wearing fitted like a glove and dipped low at the back. His first glimpse of her naked back nearly had him falling over his feet. The wide skirt of the dress ended just about her knee, leaving those tantalizing perfectly formed calves bare. What had nearly brought him to his knees, though, were the pair of impossibly high, nude heels she was wearing. Her legs looked even longer, making it difficult to look anywhere else.

For so long, his only concern had been the happiness of his two sisters. It had been his idea to cross borders and relocate. Sacramento hadn't been home any longer. Their parents' untimely death, Vivian's problems with her boss at the hospital where she'd worked, and the fact that Annie's fiancé called off their wedding weeks before the big day, had all just been too much. It was also around the same time he'd realized the cut-throat world of finance wasn't for him.

Since they'd arrived in Marietta, he hadn't even looked at a woman, let alone dated anyone. Then this redhead walked into his sister's B and B in February, irritating him, infuriating him, but as he'd just realized, also intriguing him.

Up until now, he'd managed to ignore the tightening of his body whenever he saw her, blaming it on his nonexistent love life. Now though, listening to this particular song while he was so close to her that he could count the few freckles over her nose, was making it very difficult to ignore his reaction to her.

"I…" She frowned. "You have one brown eye and one blue one. I've never noticed that before."

Nodding, he swung her around. "You've never looked at me before. It's called heterochromia."

"So that's what's been bothering me…" she murmured. "You see heaven and earth at the same time."

The last words were so soft he had to bend down to hear what she was saying. "What do you mean?"

"There's a myth—if you're born with one blue and one brown eye, you can see heaven and earth at the same time. Ghost eyes, they're called. Eyes say a lot about a person, you know. They're not called mirrors of the soul for nothing."

"That so?"

"The study of physiognomy, an old science that originated in China, claims it's possible to read information about a person's character and temperament by merely looking at his or her outward appearance. The Western world sometimes calls it junk science, but even though many scientists doubt the validity of the research on the topic, studies have found a correlation between a person's character or personality and his or her outer appearance. I find it an interesting idea. We do form instantaneous impressions of others from their facial appearance."

"So, what do you look at when you form an opinion of someone?"

"There are many different basic elements used to determine hidden meanings and traits in a person. The shape of one's face, for instance, reveals quite a lot. Someone with a high brow is usually intelligent and has an affinity for the arts. For me, the eyes in particular are a way to determine a person's character. The shape, the color…"

"Yeah? So what does the color of my eyes tell you about me?"

"I don't know you well enough to know whether you're predominantly blue-eyed or brown-eyed. There's a difference. The energy of blue is very strong—people with blue eyes tend to be uncontrollable… Come to think of it, I've seen you lose control a few times. If you're more of a brown-eyed person, you'll have great leadership qualities. People drain you; they're like energy vampires. When in love, brown-eyed people are very sensual…" Her eyes widened ever so slightly.

The word hung heavy in the air around then.

Make a joke, lighten the mood. Quickly.

Forcing out a chuckle, he swung her away from him before pulling her back into his arms. "I think I prefer the ordinary explanation of the word *heterochromia*. *Hetero* means different in ancient Greek and *chroma* color."

Those blue eyes rested steadily on him. "Just about sums up the difference between us."

Talking was good; it helped him to ignore his reaction to her nearness. "You mean the fact that you rely on myths and I on facts?"

"Some things can't be explained by only relying on facts."

"Like what?"

Sighing, she rolled her eyes. "And there you go, scowling again."

"I'm not scowling."

"You've been scowling all day."

"How do you know? You've never once looked at me."

"Of course, I've looked at you. I had to take your picture a number of times, if I recall."

"That doesn't count."

I love you, crooned the lead singer.

The slight flicker in Riley's eyes was the only indication she'd also heard the words.

"I think Barry has left or has finally passed out or someone has taken him home," she said, looking over his shoulder. "We can stop dancing now."

"The song hasn't quite finished." Without any conscious decision, he slipped both his arms around her body, slowing down their movements.

He should've let her walk away. Hell, he should've pushed her away.

After lifting her arms, she circled his neck. Soft curves fitted perfectly against his body. Ignoring the voice screaming loudly somewhere, warning him to step away, he bent down his head. *This is such a bad idea*, a little voice was yelling. Think of the potential mess if he were to give in to his instincts. His sisters were married to her cousin and brother—complicated didn't begin to describe it.

For once, though, he ignored the voice and, with his senses steeped in her scent, her long, silky hair everywhere, he buried his face in her neck.

Chapter Two

RILEY'S FEET WERE moving, but her mind had collapsed, her breathing just about stopped, and she was running on instinct. She hadn't expected Mitch to pull her closer. She hadn't expected Mitch, full stop. Big and sexy and smiling. Touching her. Dancing with her. Smiling at her. Awakening feelings she hadn't experienced in a while. Truth be told, nothing she'd ever experienced before had prepared her for being up close and personal with Mitch Miller.

Her breasts were heavy, aching with an unknown, urgent need; her heart was just about jumping out of her body. And never mind butterflies in her tummy—a whole freaking zoo had been let loose in there.

They were barely moving. Mitch's hot breath against her neck, the feeling of his obvious reaction to her, had her shivering in his arms.

"Damn it, Riley," he growled and, muttering under his breath, he steered her outside.

Gulping in cooler air, Riley tried to clear her head. The music, the laughter, the noise from inside the hotel faded.

An overwhelming instinct was urging her to drag his

head down and kiss him. Alarmed at her own thoughts, she quickly dropped her arms. Where had that come from? She didn't even like the guy.

Forcing a grin on her face, she stepped back. "And then you had to go and spoil it all by frowning again. Thanks for the dance, Mitch."

"Don't you think we should talk?"

"About what?"

"About what has just happened."

"We danced, Mitch. That was it."

His jaw was tightly clenched. "You dance like that with every man?"

"I don't go out dancing much these days."

"You know what I mean, damn it."

Sighing, she tucked a piece of her hair behind her ear. "We've danced closely. We've reacted to one another. It's biology."

His eyebrows rose. "Really? Biology."

"Yes, biology. You're an attractive man; I'm a woman; we've danced. Bodies react. Hormones, dopamine levels going silly—all can be explained."

"I thought some things can't be explained by only relying on facts."

"Well, in this case, there is a perfectly logical explanation for what has just happened between… between us." She couldn't prevent the slight shiver down her spine. "You're a very attractive man."

The small smile around his mouth was the only indication he'd seen her reaction. "Do you normally react this way when you're close to someone?"

"As I've said, I don't go out much. I haven't been with anyone since Dylan was born." As soon as the words left her mouth, she realized what she'd said.

Again, those eyebrows rose, this time even higher. "How old is Dylan?"

"Nearly four. But that is so not the point. I'd probably react to just about any man this way."

"Even Barry?"

She rolled her eyes. "Okay, except Barry. Can we now please change the subject?"

"I still think we should talk about it."

"To what end? It's not as if anything can happen between us, ever. If you haven't heard the story yet, I was literally jilted at the altar three… nearly four years ago. At the same time, I lost the very well-paying job as photographer I had at a magazine in Portland. And, oh, that was just before I found out I was pregnant. My life kinda fell apart. I have a son; I've been without a steady job for three years, but I'm finally at the point where, with Aiden and Craig's help, I have a home for Dylan and myself. I can breathe more easily. Quiet and calm—that's what I need—not complications. What happened just now? Chalk it up to the wedding, the wine, the dancing, the song—my mom's favorite, by the way—but none of it is real. Tomorrow morning in the bright light of day, this… whatever it is, would be gone."

"You sure about that?"

She nodded. "Of course, I'm sure. Besides we're practically family, and we don't even like each other. The few times I've seen you, you've been either frowning or yelling or both."

Putting out a hand, he lightly touched her hair. "Oh, I like you, Riley with the red hair. That has never been the problem. And just to be clear—we're not related. I am not your brother or your cousin."

For one crazy moment, she had the overwhelming urge to turn her face into his hand. A loud laugh from inside the hotel quickly brought her out of the near stupor she was in. Stepping back, she forced out a laugh. "Having been jilted has one advantage—I don't look at the world through rose-colored glasses anymore."

By the time she'd finished speaking, he was frowning again. "You're a beautiful woman, Riley; one would have to be dead not to notice, and I'm not dead. But I've kept my distance because of all the reasons you've just listed, and I was happy to watch from afar. But now… we've crossed a line. I've touched you, and all I can think of is kissing you."

His words fell onto her skin. Kissing. Nearly panicking, she motioned wildly with her hands. "Nothing happened, okay? A lack of sex and overactive hormones—that's the only reason we've… become aware of one another. When did you last have sex?"

The moment the words left her mouth, she'd wished she'd shut up. There was a light in those two extraordinary eyes that she'd never seen before.

"It's been a while for me, too. I haven't been interested before tonight. Do let me know in the bright light of day how you feel. That guy, the one who left you at the altar? He's an idiot. I hope you know that. Good night, Riley. It's been… interesting." Turning around, he walked back into the hotel.

GRABBING HOLD OF a chair to keep her upright, Riley watched as Mitch walked away. Her knees were literally shaking. Wow, that was so close. Her whole body was shivering with a need she'd never experienced before.

Rubbing her arms, she inhaled shakily. If the first attractive guy she danced with had this effect on her, it was definitely time to start dating again. She focused on her breathing while she tried to clear her befuddled mind, slowed down her heartbeat.

"Coz? Everything okay?" Craig asked from behind her.

Putting a smile on her face, she turned to face her cousin. "I'm fine. Shouldn't you be dancing with your bride?"

"I was, but I saw you with Mitch—has he done anything to upset you?"

"No… no. He saved me from having to dance with that

old guy who's been making a nuisance of himself."

"Barry? Sorry about that. Apparently, he was at the bar and stumbled in here by mistake. I've asked someone to take him home. You sure you're okay?"

"I'm totally fine. I'm just getting my breath back—go dance and enjoy your party."

"In a minute. You and I haven't had a chance to talk; you arrived only yesterday. I heard you also got the assignment to do the winter fashion shoot for the same magazine you worked for earlier. I'm so happy for you."

"Thank you. That's why I arrived so late." She smiled. "There were several things to finalize before I could get on a plane."

"Working freelance isn't easy, but it seems you're now my sought-after photographer cousin."

"I can't tell you how grateful and relieved I am things are going so well. I'm fully booked for fashion shoots until next year this time, I'm happy to say. Thanks to my inheritance and the way you and Aiden always pitched in to help with Dylan, I was always more than fine, but I'm finally at a place where I can relax ever so slightly."

Craig touched her arm. "Please remember both Aiden and I will be visiting Portland regularly for work, so do let us know if you need help with Dylan? Will you be able to find someone to look after him when you're working?"

Riley nodded. "Fortunately, he's starting prekindergarten in September. That would make things much easier. But thanks, coz, I promise to let you know. Now go and dance with your bride."

Breathing out slowly, Riley followed her cousin back into the hotel. Everything was going to be all right. She hadn't done anything stupid, so she could relax. And bonus, Dylan and she were only staying another night.

Once she was back in Portland, she'd be too busy to remember anything that had happened here tonight.

After this incident, one thing was clear, though—she seriously needed to get out more, accept invitations to parties, try dating apps or whatever it was single women did these days. If her body reacted this way to the first sexy guy she'd been close to in nearly four years, it was becoming quite urgent.

MITCH WALKED BLINDLY toward the bar. He wasn't much of a drinker, but maybe a glass of wine would help dull the ache in his belly.

Damn it, he shouldn't have danced with Riley. He'd known she was trouble the moment he'd laid eyes on those long, red curls, killer body, and saucy smile of hers way back in February. She'd never been around for long, and during the times she'd been here, they'd barely spoken. She'd teased him mercilessly when he'd been upset with the damn O'Sullivans sniffing around his sisters, but otherwise, they hadn't spent time together. What he couldn't have predicted was the way his body would react to her closeness.

He'd never had a reason to touch her before. But then she'd grabbed his hand, telling him to dance with her. Also, he hadn't been the only one affected by their closeness. He'd heard her soft gasp, saw her breasts straining against the soft material of her dress. *Damn it, Miller, this isn't helping.*

"Mitch!" someone called from the table he was passing.

It was Janice: Riley, Mitch, and Craig's godmother. She was his colleague; they were both teachers at the local high school. She beckoned him closer.

"Everything okay?" he asked as he neared the older woman.

She got up. "I need to go to the bathroom, quickly. Would you mind keeping an eye on Dylan?" Grinning, she lifted the tablecloth. "How anyone can sleep in this noise, I have no idea, but he's not moving. I won't be long."

Taking a chair next to Janice's, Mitch nodded as he too lifted the tablecloth to watch the little boy sleep. He'd never realized it before, but since he'd walked away from his previous life as a chartered accountant at a big bank in Sacramento and started teaching at Marietta High School nearly two years ago, he'd discovered he liked children. There was something endearing about them, even behind the toughest teenager. You just needed time and patience to reach the soul behind the mask of anger.

As he watched, Dylan opened his eyes. "Mitch?" he asked sleepily. "Where's Mommy?"

"She's close by. Go back to sleep, I'm here."

"You're not yelling?"

Solemnly, Mitch shook his head. "No yelling. Now go back to sleep."

But Dylan got up, and with his blanket trailing behind him, he climbed onto Mitch's lap. Within minutes, he'd curled up against Mitch's body and was asleep again.

Something warm opened up inside Mitch. Leaning back, he put his knee on his leg to make more room for the little boy and cuddled him. It would be nice to someday have his own…

Frowning, he stared down at the boy. Where did that come from? Marriage and children hadn't been things he'd ever thought about before. A little girl with red hair and her mom's lavender-blue eyes…

"What are you doing?" Riley asked from behind him.

Mitch looked up as Riley rushed closer, her eyes clouded with worry.

"Janice went to the bathroom."

She relaxed visibly. "I'll take him now. We have to go anyway."

She moved to take the boy from him, but Mitch got up, still holding the little boy in his arms. "I'll go with you and help…"

Grabbing her bag, Riley's eyes narrowed. "I'm quite capable of carrying my own son."

"I know. I can help, though."

"Okay, fine. But just to the car."

Chapter Three

When Riley stopped in front of Aunt Janice's house, she was still blinking back tears. The gentle way in which Mitch had put her son in the car, had grabbed her at the throat and wouldn't let go.

Percy, Dylan's dad, hadn't wanted to have anything to do with him. When she'd found out she was pregnant weeks after being dumped at the altar, she'd contacted her ex, hoping he'd at least acknowledge his child. But with a few scathing remarks, he'd walked away.

Frowning, she got out of the car. She should've listened to her gut and trusted her instincts telling her Percy's eyes were way too close-set, a clear sign of someone with a weak will. Not a mistake she'd make again. Trust her gut was her motto these days and what her gut was telling her… no screaming at her, was to get back to Portland as soon as possible.

She had thought of extending her stay with Aunt Janice for another day or two, but it was more than clear she had to get away from here, away from Mitch Miller as soon as possible. Having another encounter, however innocent, with him was something she had to avoid at all costs.

This morning when she'd woken up, Mitch hadn't even been on her radar, let alone someone who could make her dopamine levels go crazy. But after dancing with him, touching his broad shoulders, feeling his body close to hers… Oh, damn, she shouldn't be thinking about him, seriously.

Closing her eyes, she could still feel his warm hand on her skin; hear his ragged breathing in her neck. Groaning out loud, she opened the door. This was not helping.

As she got out of the car, another car pulled up behind hers. Even before she'd closed the car door she knew—it was Mitch. She'd told him she'd be able to get Dylan into her aunt's house all by herself, but of course he didn't listen.

Inhaling deeply, she tried to calm herself as he walked toward her. She hated any form of confrontation.

"Why are you here, Mitch?"

He didn't answer her, just opened the back door of her car and picked up Dylan.

"I told you I can handle it."

"I know you're quite capable of doing everything yourself; you've made that clear. But I'm here; I can help. Let me."

Cross, she stared at his back as he walked toward the front door. It was very difficult to stay angry with someone who was going out of his way to help her son.

Well, she didn't have to like it. Stomping past him, she

unlocked the front door and quickly walked toward the room where Aunt Janice had made a bed for Dylan. She switched on the light in the corridor and opened the blanket so that Mitch could put her son down.

With infinite care, Mitch crouched lower and placed Dylan on the bed. She waited for him to leave, but he first pulled the blanket over her son before he turned away and walked out of the room.

Exhaling slowly, she kissed Dylan's forehead before she also headed out.

Mitch was waiting at the front door.

"Thank you," she got out.

"When are you leaving?"

"Tomorrow."

Nodding, he opened the door. "Lock the door behind me."

"Seriously. I don't need you looking after me as well. I have a brother and a cousin, I don't—"

That was as far as she got. The next moment, a big hand cupped her face. "I'm very glad I'm neither your brother nor your cousin," he said before he lowered his head.

She should move, push him away, say something, but instead, she watched, stunned, as his lips came closer and closer until their mouths were nearly touching.

"If you don't want me to kiss you, now's the time to push me away," he murmured, his eyes roaming over her face, his hot breath caressing her skin. "Did you know you have exactly three freckles on the bridge of your nose? And on this cheek there are..."

Whether it was the glass of wine she'd had earlier, the song they'd danced to still running through her mind or the heat from Mitch's body, she didn't know, but ignoring the near hysterical voice warning her to step away, she lifted herself on her toes.

Mitch's eyes flashed once before his mouth covered hers.

His lips were hot, urgent, and within seconds, she was clinging to him, desperately worried he'd stopped. Angling his head, he deepened the kiss, and as if she'd done it a hundred times before, she stepped in between his legs.

His body was made for hers was her last coherent thought before Mitch's tongue shot through to the depths of her mouth where hers was eagerly waiting for the dance.

Warm hands slid over her back, molding her against him, but it wasn't enough; she needed to touch him to become a part of him...

Shocked, she pulled her head away. His eyes had darkened, both the blue and brown eyes nearly black with desire as he gasped for breath.

"This is crazy," she got out. "You have to go."

He slid his hands down her arms. "Is that really what you want?"

Finally, sanity prevailed. Hastily, she stepped back. "Yes, it is. I'm going to forget this ever happened. I suggest you do the same."

"Forget I kissed you?"

"Blame it on the night, the romance of a wedding..."

"The wine, the music?" he asked, not bothering to hide the sarcasm.

"Exactly. Good night, Mitch. Thank you for your help."

Opening the door, she waited for him to leave.

She was just about to close the door when he spoke again. "What if we don't?"

"Don't what?"

"Forget about the kiss?"

Without answering him, she closed the door. She waited there until she could hear the engine of his car fade away.

Nearly frantic, she ran to her room and pulled the suitcase out she'd brought along. That... whatever that was, could never happen again. The day before, Mitch had only been someone who mildly irritated her—now...

Inhaling deeply, she tried to clear her head. She was not going to think about Mitch one second longer. She and Dylan were leaving first thing tomorrow. In Portland, a whole new life was waiting for them.

MITCH THREW HIS car keys on the only table in his house. He couldn't go back to the wedding; he needed time to clear his head.

Still freaked out by the powerful feelings Riley

O'Sullivan had stirred up in him, he paced his sparsely furnished living room. Damn, she was right—it probably was the whole wedding atmosphere that had them both become aware of each other. She reckoned all would be forgotten in the bright light of day. Hopefully, she was right.

He bumped into one of the boxes standing around, hurting his big toe. Cussing, he kicked the box before he sighed. The obvious solution would be to find time to unpack.

When he and Vivian had moved in with Annie in the B and B she'd bought when they'd arrived in Marietta, he'd known at some point he'd move out and buy his own place. That his two sisters would get married within seventeen months after their arrival in Marietta, had not been something he'd expected, though.

Fortunately, he'd found this house on the corner of Collier and First Street, close to where Annie and Vivian were living. Like the houses his sisters had bought, it was also an old house, but the fact that it had already been renovated, had made his decision to buy it easy.

He'd just moved in at the beginning of this week. He put a bed and table in one of the upstairs bedrooms, the place he used the most at the moment. The rest of his life was still packed up in all the boxes standing around the house.

The main reason he'd wanted to leave his very well-paid job in a big bank back in Sacramento, was to write the novel that had been on his mind since he'd left school. A few short stories he'd written had made it out into the world, but it was only after his parents' untimely death, he'd known it was time to take the leap to make sure he'd have more time to write. Life was short, unpredictable, as he'd discovered, and if he wanted to be a writer, he should be writing.

The leap had been taken: they were all here; he was teaching math so that he could write. Everything sounded perfect, except… he wasn't writing.

He'd always been fascinated by history, and initially, he'd thought to write something set around the time Sacramento city was founded. The original location caused the city to be periodically filled with water. Fires would also sweep through the city, and the sidewalks and buildings had to be raised. Wooden structures were replaced with stronger materials like brick and stone.

A story about a nightclub owner's struggle to survive during this time had steadily been taking shape in his subconscious, long before their move to Marietta. Over the past seventeen months, he'd been trying to work out the plot. He had a big board filled with empty yellow stickers; he simply hadn't been able to get past chapter one.

As he stared at the row of still unpacked boxes, an idea that had popped into his head in February, and one he'd studiously been ignoring up to now, again floated through his mind. Damn it, maybe he should listen to the irritating voice in his head and start from scratch.

The first time he'd heard Janice mention Marietta's history, his original story had begun to fade and his thoughts had shifted in a completely different direction. Janice also told them about the history of Grey's Saloon. Nowadays, the saloon served food and drink—there might be the occasional fight—but all in all, it was quite a reputable place to dine at. Back in the day, however, things had been very different.

Ephraim Grey had started the saloon when he'd arrived in the area during the 1880s. Rumor had it, in an effort to escape some trouble back in Boston, he'd even left his family behind. His son and heir, Josiah, used to run a bordello in the upstairs rooms.

This was the information that had triggered another what-if question, one that wouldn't let go. What if someone else had arrived, in Marietta… Alfred Cooper? The name came out of nowhere. He had a daughter, Dorothy, and together, they opened another saloon around the same time. A few months later, though, his daughter disappeared…

He raced up the stairs two at a time. He wasn't going to sleep anyway; he might as well try to write.

A few moments later, he was in front of his open computer. For a moment, the subtle scent of orange blossoms floated around him. Cussing softly, he dropped his hands on the keyboard and began typing, the clean, yellow stickers on the board in front of him forgotten.

Walking through the swing doors of the new saloon in town, Joshua Lewis took off his hat.

A sultry voice stopped him in his tracks. "You'll be welcome here when you get rid of the mud on your boots."

A slender figure stepped out of the shadows. In one glance, he took in everything about her—from her long, fiery-red tresses, startling blue eyes, saucy smile, to the slim hand resting on her hip, her whole demeanor challenging him to argue with her.

Stunned by the words simply flowing out of him, Mitch leaned back in his chair for a moment. But the urgency to continue didn't give him much time to ponder about what he was writing.

His hands dropped, and his fingers flew over the keyboard.

He was writing.

IT WAS LATE afternoon on Sunday before Riley and Dylan finally got home. Dylan had been a champ, but the nearly hour-long layover in Seattle, before embarking on the last leg to Portland so close after their flight to Bozeman on Friday, seemed to have taken its toll on her son.

Carrying Dylan, while dragging their suitcase behind her, she gritted her teeth. She was a thoroughly modern twenty-first century woman, happy and capable of slaying dragons all by herself, *thank you very much*. It was just sometimes, like now, it would've been nice to have someone help her. As Mitch had done…

What the—Exasperated, she nearly tripped over herself and quickly dropped the suitcase so that she could unlock the front door to her house. Mitch O'Sullivan seemed to have ingrained himself into her thoughts, and she had no idea how to get rid of him.

Her phone bleeped—probably Aunt Janice, but she first wanted to put Dylan down. Minutes later, she closed her son's door behind her. He'd hardly stirred as she put him down and would probably sleep for another hour. She should order food; Dylan would be hungry when he woke up. She hadn't eaten much either during the long trip.

Rolling her shoulders, she tried to relax. Being cooped up with lots of other people all day had drained her. Normally, she stayed away from large crowds. She even did her shopping later in the day when most other people were already home.

Taking a deep breath, she clicked on her phone as she walked back to the living room to fetch the suitcase. Looking around her, she willed herself to relax. The calm, muted colors of the walls and furniture usually helped her to regain her equilibrium after a day engaging with other people. Strangely, though, her shoulders stayed stiff, the knot in her tummy refusing to let go. Something was bothering her.

Deep in thought, she opened her messages and stilled. There was a message from Aunt Janice, yes, but that wasn't the only message. There was also one from Mitch.

With her eyes on her phone, her breath stuck somewhere in her throat, she sat down on the nearest chair. Slowly exhaling, she opened the message.

Still want to kiss you. The bright light of day hasn't changed that.

It took a few minutes to realize two things—one, she was smiling like an idiot, and two, her heart was beating like a runaway train.

Quickly putting down her phone, she jumped up and began pacing.

Damn it, he was right—the bright light of day hadn't changed a thing. Over the last twenty hours, she'd hardly thought of anything else but Mitch's kiss, his warm body close to hers, his brown and blue eyes on hers, but most of all—her unexpected reaction to him.

Surely this craziness wouldn't last; it couldn't last. She didn't even like the guy. He was forever yelling or frowning or both, and after Percy, she'd done her best to keep her life drama-free.

In all fairness, though, Mitch was nothing like Percy. She just had to remember the gentle way he was with her son to know that.

But… if one dance with Mitch Miller made her feel this way, imagine what spending more time with him would to do her equilibrium.

The hopelessness she'd experienced the week she'd been dumped at the altar, lost her job, found out she was pregnant, and discovered Percy had cleaned out their joint bank account, had been devastating. The only one other time in her life she'd felt like that was when first, their dad had died while she was still at school, and then a year later, her mother. That was when Aunt Janice had moved in with them, bringing some calm back into the household with her.

Since she'd discovered she was pregnant, her goal had been to try to create a peaceful environment for her son, one reminiscent of her own happy childhood. Craig and Aiden had both tried to get her to move in with them, but she needed a place to call her own, a place where she could escape from other people's drama. She was never again going to rely on someone else to provide for her or her son; trusting someone else beside her family wasn't a mistake she'd make again.

Aiden and Craig had been there for her every step of the way, though, insisting on helping. Craig had even moved in with her for a few months to help with Dylan. Fortunately, those first harrowing months with a small baby were behind her, she had a new job, Dylan was going to start prekindergarten, and her life was finally as she'd wanted it.

She was not throwing away her peace of mind because a devastatingly attractive guy had kissed her.

Picking up her phone, she quickly wrote a text. Deleted it. Wrote another one. Deleted it. She threw her phone down again.

There was nothing to say. She could tell him she hadn't stopped thinking about their kiss. She could tell him about all the forgotten feelings he'd stirred up; she could ask him how she was supposed to forget those few moments of bliss with him, but she wouldn't.

Picking up her phone again, she stared at the small

screen. Maybe... maybe she could type out the words and not send the text. At least that way she'd get it off her chest and could maybe put the whole thing behind her.

Sitting down, she wrote a text to Mitch. After she'd finished, she put her phone down again.

He would never know how very close she'd come to making a huge mistake.

Chapter Four

FOUR MONTHS LATER, Riley stared open-mouthed at the photos on her computer screen. Alarmed, she closed the folder and the program before she jumped up and began pacing. How did this happen?

Her brief as the photographer on Craig and Annie's wedding at the beginning of August had been clear. She had to take pictures of the happy couple—that had been her job. The focus had been supposed to be on them, their joy, what they did during the day, so what went wrong?

Taking a deep breath, she tried to calm herself. There had to be some mistake; she had probably opened the wrong folder. *Deep breaths, O'Sullivan, deep breaths.* It was Thursday evening, the last week of November, Dylan was already in bed, and she had to finish editing the wedding photos today so that she could finally send them to her cousin and his wife.

She'd been postponing doing this since she and Dylan had arrived back from Marietta. There had been many good reasons why she'd been putting it off.

The past four months had been crazy. Beside the normal

requests for fashion shoots, she'd also received more and more invitations over the last few months to take part in exhibitions in galleries. It had never been something she'd even considered, but maybe she should try.

Earlier this year, she'd even had an invitation from a gallery in Bozeman to take part in an exhibition they were having over Christmas. They were looking for portraits, not really her thing, but it was nice to be recognized. Apparently, the owner had seen her work in a magazine and was hoping she'd be interested.

Not only had she been busy, she also hadn't realized how much she would miss both Aiden and Craig. Before they'd both moved to Marietta, they'd often dropped by to help with Dylan or share a meal. She had also always been able to rely on them to step in and watch Dylan if she had to be somewhere for a shoot.

Both her brother and cousin had touched base in Portland for work over the last eighteen weeks and, accompanied by Vivian and Annie, had spent time with her and Dylan. It had been hard to say goodbye each time; she really missed having her family close by.

It was strange not having Dylan around her all day. On top of that, she was worried about him. He was normally a happy little boy who loved making friends, and she'd thought he would like school, but after nearly four months, he was still dragging his feet when they left for school in the morning. Obviously, he wasn't very happy. It was probably just a phase. It had been an adjustment for both of them, but if this continued, she'd have to go and see his teacher. Hopefully soon, Dylan would be excited to go to school.

It was hard raising a child on her own. Even with the help of her cousin and brother, when they'd both still been living in Portland, there had been days she'd felt like getting into Dylan's cot with him and joined in his crying. With time and patience and remembering her own mom, she'd learned how to be the best mom she could be.

She had a son, a home, and a job, and if she could just figure out how to *do* this school thing, she could be quite happy and busy and not keep thinking about Mitch Miller and his kiss.

It had been four months, seriously. Surely, she should've been so over the freaking kiss by now.

The whole incident was, even if she hadn't wanted to acknowledge it, of course, the reason she'd kept putting off editing the wedding photographs. It was too soon after her encounter with Mitch, and she simply couldn't look at pictures reminding her of that night, of the kiss.

Four months later, though, she was still waking up, gasping for air after another steamy dream about him. For goodness' sake, the man had counted her freckles—why was she still hung up on him?

Annie, her new sister-in-law, had said they were happy to wait for the wedding photos until she was done, but she knew they had to be keen to see pictures of their big day.

Today was going to be the day she'd do the editing and maybe then she'd be able to finally forget someone like Mitch Miller existed.

That was before she'd known what she'd done, though. Slowing down, she sat down in front of her computer again. Okay, she'd try again. There had to be some mistake, surely...

She'd imported the photos from her camera on to her laptop just after she'd arrived back from Marietta in August.

Again, she opened the imaging and graphic design software program on which she edited her photos. Maybe she hadn't looked at the correct folder. Maybe she'd stored the original photos in more than one folder or something.

Quickly scanning through the folders on the computer's desktop, she held her breath. She didn't normally make mistakes when doing her job, but she'd still been so rattled by Mitch's kiss when she and Dylan had arrived back in Portland, it was entirely possible she'd done something stupid when she'd saved the photos. Oh, damn, not the words of the freaking song again.

Minutes later, she sat back, staring at her laptop. She hadn't made a mistake. There were photos of Craig and Annie, yes. Beautiful photos, in fact. And as she'd predicted, the one she'd taken as Craig had touched Annie's face, was exactly as perfect as she'd hoped it would be.

What she hadn't known until now, though, was that most of the photos she'd taken during the course of the day were of Mitch Miller. Mitch, smiling at his sisters, Mitch in front of Annie while she fastened his tie, Mitch coming down the aisle with Annie, Mitch dancing with Aunt Janice, Mitch with her son, Mitch talking with other guests, Mitch with his jacket, Mitch without his jacket—hundreds of photos of Mitch.

Dropping her hands back on her laptop, she scrolled through the rest of the pictures. At the next one, she froze. Another picture of Mitch filled the screen. Stunned, her heart beating at an alarming rate, she leaned back in her chair and stared.

She'd caught Mitch in a moment he'd been staring directly at the camera, at her. What was the expression in his eyes, though? It wasn't one she'd ever seen before, or one she'd picked up in any of the other pictures of him. There was a message in those eyes, but for the life of her, she couldn't figure out what it was.

Her hands shaking, she continued scrolling. Minutes later, she dropped her head in her hands.

What was freaking her out more than anything else was the fact that these photos had all been taken before she'd danced with him, before he'd kissed her, before she'd become aware of him.

What did that mean? Did it mean anything? Or was it one of those strange things, as she'd told Mitch, that couldn't be explained by relying on mere facts?

Staring at the photos of Mitch, she tilted her head, trying

to look at it critically. These were all fabulous photos even if she'd taken them herself—she could see that. The camera settings, compositions, angles, lightning, backdrops—all had been perfect in the moments she'd caught Mitch unguarded. More importantly, though, she'd captured emotive portraits that would touch anyone looking at them in one way or another.

She was seeing a whole different Mitch to the one she'd seen over the last few months.

Look at this one… She clicked on the photo, enlarging it. This one she'd taken outside before they'd entered the hotel. Mitch had crouched down to talk to Dylan. Although she'd focused on them, the gorgeous cottonwood tree with bright yellow leaves behind them formed the perfect, blurry backdrop.

Mitch was relaxed, smiling—she'd never seen him looking like this. How could she have taken this photo and not have remembered it? How could she have taken hundreds of photos of him and not remembered?

As she looked at his face, she slowly became aware of other elements she should've noticed before. His eyebrows, for instance, pointed downward. According to physiognomy, this usually indicated the person was kind, generous, and always straightforward. His high forehead suggested intelligence, yes, but also confidence, maturity, practical and good financial management skills.

The end of his lips pointed upward, which suggested he

was positive, cheerful, and friendly. Not that she'd seen much of that, but okay, he'd been worried about his sisters. She'd also seen how gentle he could be with her son, how caring.

Going back to the pictures, she clicked on the next one to enlarge it, as well. It had been taken just after Mitch had left Annie with Craig at the altar. Riley sat back, staring at the picture.

This moment she actually remembered. She'd been quite close to the front and had captured the moment Craig had taken Annie's hand. Craig hadn't waited for anyone to tell him what to do; he'd bent his head and kissed his bride under whistles and clapping. Seconds later, Mitch was walking back to take his place next to Aunt Janice. She'd caught him in the moment as he was turning away from his sister.

And look at that—Mitch actually had tears in his eyes. She hadn't seen that when she'd taken the photo. He was smiling crookedly, but the brightness in his eyes, her camera had picked up, were unmistakably tears.

The zoo in her tummy was going ballistic; her heart was beating frantically, completely out of control. If a picture of Mitch could do this to her, what would happen if she were to see him again?

Nearly panicking, she inhaled deeply. These were all worthy to be shown in an exhibition, but she'd have to delete the lot. Nobody, but nobody, could ever know she'd taken these.

Quickly, she went back to the folder, but her finger hovered over the first picture of Mitch. Damn it, these were so good, she couldn't delete them.

Within seconds, she'd created a new folder. Name? Normally, nobody else ever used her laptop, but her cousin and brother had on occasion opened her laptop to look at her work. She wouldn't want either of them to open this and see what she was hiding in it, so she needed a name that wouldn't interest them.

From nowhere, an idea popped into her head. Rolling her eyes at her own silliness, she quickly named the folder. *Okay, done. Time to move on.*

Minutes later, the imaging and graphic design software program was open again. She was ready to edit the wedding pictures. There were still a few pictures of Mitch; he was, after all, the bride's brother, the one who had walked her down the aisle. Nobody would find it strange that she'd taken pictures of him. What everyone would find very strange, though, was the whole folder of pictures of Mitch.

As she worked, her heartbeat finally slowed down.

Her phone rang. It was Aunt Janice. Hesitating a moment, she rubbed her face. Their aunt had an uncanny way of knowing things they'd rather she didn't know. Sighing, she answered. Aunt Janice had been there at a time Riley had needed her most; she'd walk over hot coals for her. She could never not answer a call from her aunt.

"Aunt Janice, it's so nice to hear from you," she greeted.

"Hello, my dear," her aunt said, sounding strange.

"Aunt Janice? Are you okay?"

"Oh, just a silly cold, sweetie—nothing to bother yourself about. Vivian has given me something. I should be fine by tomorrow. I haven't heard from you for a while. How are you? And Dylan?"

As Riley opened her mouth to answer, her aunt coughed.

"Sorry, Riley," she said, sounding tired.

"Aunt Janice, you are not well!" Riley scolded. "Are you in bed?"

"Yes, yes, I am." There was another round of coughing.

The line crackled, and Riley could barely hear what her aunt was saying.

"Stay at home…"

Riley got up quickly. "You stay put. Dylan and I will be there tomorrow. Promise me you'll stay in bed?"

"No, sweetie, that's really not necessary…"

"Of course, it is. Now drink your medicine and rest. I'll let you know when we'll land in Bozeman."

"But, Riley, you are so busy. I don't want to take you away from your work."

"I don't have another photo shoot over the next week, and editing photos I can do from anywhere."

"I really don't want to burden you…"

"You'll never be a burden, Aunt Janice, you know that. See you tomorrow."

Minutes later, Riley was on her phone, looking for flights. Aunt Janice should've called her sooner, and why hadn't Craig or Aiden told her their aunt was ill?

Groaning, she quickly booked flights for herself and Dylan. Aunt Janice wasn't the problem. She was. Because she hadn't wanted to hear anything about Mitch, she hadn't spoken to Aunt Janice or her brother or cousin in a while. She was the only one to blame.

MITCH'S FINGERS WERE flying over the keys of his computer. The words were flowing; he didn't hesitate once. There was an urgency inside of him, pressuring him to finish the story. It was Thursday night, and he was nearing the point where he could write THE END.

The story he'd started on the night of Craig and Annie's wedding had moved in a direction he couldn't have foreseen four months ago. Initially, he'd wasted precious time trying to keep to some kind of structure. He'd quickly discovered writing didn't work that way. At least, not for him.

Over the past few months, he'd learned to trust the voices in his head, he'd learned not to try and force something on the characters they didn't want to do, and he'd learned to rely on the mysterious workings of the subconscious. Things happened in there while he was sleeping.

What he hadn't foreseen was that grief would somehow

invade his story as one of the main themes. It hadn't even been something he'd thought about, or rather, he hadn't known it had been on his mind. He hadn't known he was still grieving for his parents.

After all this time, he still vividly remembered the moment he'd heard they were gone. His dad had accompanied his mother, a social worker, when she'd visited a client on the wrong side of town. A spray of bullets from a drive-by shooting, meant for someone else, had killed both of them.

The feeling of despair and hopelessness he'd experienced then, he'd buried deep. His sisters had needed him, and he hadn't been able to fall apart—he'd needed to be able to help them. Turned out, he'd discovered while writing this story, grief refused to be buried. It had to be dealt with. Writing the story that had been mulling in his mind for so long had given him an opportunity to do just that.

What had probably surprised him the most, though, was the way he'd ended up describing the daughter of the protagonist, Alfred Cooper. He didn't need a psychologist to explain to him why Dorothy had red hair, blue eyes, and a body that left men drooling over her.

Chuckling, he rubbed his tired eyes. He was still lusting after Riley O'Sullivan. That was why. And that damn kiss? He went to bed thinking about Riley's soft lips, and every single morning he woke up with the same thought, his body on fire for her. And he hadn't touched a drop of alcohol since she'd left.

Writing in August had been easy. It had still been school holidays, but since school had started at the end of August, the only time he'd had to write was during the night and the odd weekend when there hadn't been any school sport he'd needed to attend.

Writing had also effectively prevented him from doing something stupid like getting on a plane to visit Riley and Dylan. Damn it, he missed her. He'd thought she'd have made a trip to Marietta to see her family again by now, but since she'd left the day after the wedding, he hadn't seen or heard from her.

She hadn't replied to the text he'd sent her the day after he'd kissed her. Not even to tell him not to text her. Just silence. Obviously, she was merrily going about her day, their kiss forgotten.

He stopped typing. Damn it, this happened every time he thought of Riley. *Focus, Miller, focus. One more paragraph.*

His fingers hovered over the keys. There were two possible endings he'd been musing over. The one was a neat ending, a happy one. The other one was more real.

Chuckling, he finished the last paragraph within minutes. He'd known which one it should be for some time. He just had to write it down.

THE END

Tired but elated, he leaned back in his chair. It was done. He'd written the story. It had taken him months, sleepless nights, many, many cups of coffee, but it was done.

Dazed, he looked around him. He still hadn't unpacked all the boxes standing around; he hadn't even furnished the rest of his house. His life had basically been put on hold over the last few months while he'd been concentrating on finishing his story.

Stretching, he got up and walked toward the window.

It was a little after midnight, his watch told him. The street below was empty, the lights strangely comforting. Here and there, a house had already been decorated for Christmas.

As he and his two sisters had discovered the previous year, folks in Marietta were big on Christmas. All sorts of activities were spread out over the weeks leading up to the actual day. The whole town was already abuzz with everything that would happen over the next few weeks.

Because he'd been so focused on his writing, he hadn't seen either of his sisters for a while. On his phone, there was an invitation from Annie to lunch on Sunday that he should respond to. She was sure to also invite Aiden and Vivian. It would be a good opportunity to find out how Riley was doing. Someone was bound to mention her.

He walked back to his chair. There was still editing to be done, but for the first time in a long time, his mind wasn't busy working out scenes.

Riley. Groaning, he closed his laptop. He wished he could turn off his thoughts about Riley as easily. What was he supposed to do about that?

Chapter Five

HER BROTHER FINALLY returned her call on Friday as Riley and Dylan drove away from Bozeman airport. It was nearly four o'clock, and Dylan's eyes were drooping. Three hours weren't that bad for a flight, but the hour-long layover in Seattle made for a long day for a four-year-old. They'd had a quick lunch at the airport before they fetched their rental car.

She'd tried to phone Aiden and Craig before they'd left Portland, but neither had picked up their phones. When they'd landed in Seattle, she'd texted both of them, asking about Aunt Janice, but so far, she hadn't heard from them.

"Hi, Riley," Aiden called out. "Sorry, I see you called me and sent a message, I've had a busy morning. We've been worried—we haven't heard from you in a while and then two calls and a text on one day."

"I've had a crazy few weeks, but seriously, Aiden, you and Craig should please let me know when Aunt Janice isn't well. She'd always been so good to us, I'm happy to drop everything to come and help her. Dylan and I have just left Bozeman airport, so we should arrive at her place in about twenty minutes' time."

"What? I don't understand. We saw her earlier in the week and she was fine."

"She called me last night—she's definitely ill. She said she'd seen Vivian…" Confused, Riley frowned.

"I have no idea what you're talking about," Aiden said, also clearly baffled. "I know she was here to see Vivian yesterday morning, but I as far as I know, she's not ill. Let me find out what's going on, though. I'll meet you at her house."

Riley stepped on the gas. She was really worried now. Maybe Aunt Janice had had a fever when they'd spoke. What if she'd passed out by now and wasn't able to contact anyone else?

MITCH WAS DRIVING back home from school on Friday when he saw his brother-in-law, Aiden, racing down the street in his car toward Janice O'Sullivan's house.

Had something happened to Janice? She'd seemed fine earlier today when he'd seen her at school.

With a quick look in his rearview mirror, he made a U-turn and followed Aiden. As he parked in front of Janice's house, Aiden was already getting out of his car.

"Is there a problem?" he asked as he got out of his car. "Has something happened to Janice?"

"I'm not sure," Aiden said as they walked toward the house. "Riley just phoned. She's on her way here. She spoke to Aunt Janice last night. According to my sister, our aunt is ill, but…"

At the mention of Riley's name, Mitch's heart kicked him in the ribs. "I saw your aunt this morning at school," Mitch said. "She looked fine then."

"Well, let's find out." Aiden knocked on the door.

Minutes later, the door flew open. A very healthy-looking Janice, dressed in bright yellow, huge earrings dangling from her ears, smiled broadly at them. "What a lovely surprise to see both of you. Come on in, please. I've just made tea."

Frowning, Aiden looked at Mitch, but he didn't say anything as they followed Janice to the kitchen. "Do sit down. Let me just get the cups."

"Aunt Janice, are you okay?" Aiden asked.

She turned to them, clearly surprised at the question. "Of course, my dear. I'm very healthy and so happy you and Craig are now also in Marietta. If we can only find a way to get Riley—"

Aiden inhaled sharply. "Aunt Janice?" he interrupted his aunt. "Please don't tell me you've faked being ill just to get Riley to visit? She's dropped everything to fly to you because she thinks you're just about dying. Damn it, are you trying your matchmaking skills again? Is that what this is all about?"

This time Janice kept her back to them as she proceeded to make the tea. "I don't know what you're going on about. I had a bit of a cough yesterday. Vivian gave me something…"

"She gave you vitamins," Aiden said. "I've spoken to her."

"Oh, sweetie, relax. I just missed Riley so much."

"Aunt Janice," Aiden said sternly. "You can't…"

The doorbell chimed.

Aunt Janice clapped her hands. "That would be Riley. Mitch, could you help with little Dylan? He's probably fallen asleep on the way here. Aiden, will you make more tea? We can drink it in the living room."

While Aiden was still scowling, Mitch followed Janice to the front door. His heart was just about jumping out of his body. Within minutes, he was going to see Riley again.

RILEY HAD DYLAN on her hip while she knocked on Aunt Janice's front door. He'd been sleeping, but she didn't want to leave him in the car. When she'd parked the rental just now, she'd recognized the two cars in the driveway. Aiden and Mitch's cars. Did the fact that they were both here mean Aunt Janice was so much worse than what she'd thought?

She should've made a point of checking up on her aunt more regularly. Even just a message. Yes, she'd been busy, but she should've made time, she should've…

She knocked again. Not quite an easy task because in front of the door was a huge Christmas wreath. Aunt Janice had always put one on the front door of their home while she'd been living with them, Riley remembered. She was clearly still going all out for Christmas. All the windows of her house facing the street were also decorated with bright Christmas lights.

The front door flew open. Aunt Janice stood there, smiling. Relief made Riley slightly dizzy for a moment. Behind her aunt Mitch appeared. Her heart sighed. It was *so* good to see him.

"Riley, sweetheart, I'm so happy you're here. I've just missed you so. Now that both Craig and Aiden are in Marietta, I even miss you more. Hello, Dylan," she said softly, touching his face. "Ahh, look at him, he's grown so big over the past four months!"

Riley was so flabbergasted, she couldn't get a word out.

Mitch stepped forward. "Hi," he said and before she knew what he would do, he bent down and kissed her. His warm lips touched hers only briefly, but she felt the kiss right down to the soles of her feet.

Gently, he took the sleepy Dylan from her. "Hi, buddy, I've missed this face." He was talking to Dylan, but his eyes were on Riley.

Inhaling deeply, she tried to clear her head. "Aunt Janice, what's going on? Last night… you were coughing, and you told me you were feeling poorly and were in bed."

Grinning, Aunt Janice reached out and pulled Riley into a hug. "Oh, sweetie, I may have exaggerated a tad, but it was time for you to visit again, don't you think? Come on in. You're here, and I'm so, so happy."

Over Aunt Janice's shoulder, she watched Mitch with Dylan. Her son had woken up and was smiling at Mitch.

"I've made more tea!" Aiden called out from the direction of the kitchen.

"Please say you're not angry with me?" Aunt Janice pleaded.

Sighing, Riley shook her head. "It's not going to make any difference, is it? You've conned me into visiting you! Next time, just tell me you want me to visit; I've been sick with worry. I couldn't get hold of Craig or Aiden to find out what was going on."

Aunt Janice took Riley's arm. "I know, and I'm sorry for worrying you, but it's not the same without you here. I haven't heard from you for a while and… well, here you are." She beamed.

Aiden came down the corridor with a tray in his hand. "Hi, sis. Dylan! How's my favorite nephew? All grown up and going to school, I hear."

"I don't like school," Dylan announced. "Mom, look—it's Christmas in the house."

Mitch put him down gently. Dylan rushed over to look at all Aunt Janice's Christmas decorations.

"I remember all of these." Riley smiled. "The nativity set,

nutcracker soldier... you still have everything."

Aunt Janice nodded. "Of course. I hope you're here long enough so that Dylan can help me decorate the tree."

"Can we, Mom? Please?" Dylan asked.

"I have to go back to work, sweetie."

Fortunately, Dylan saw another Christmas decoration and rushed off.

Aiden put his arm around Riley. His eyes twinkled. "You do know why you've been conned into visiting Marietta?"

"What do you mean?"

"Aunt Janice isn't quite satisfied yet. Although both Craig and I have fallen for two local beauties, you're still unattached. She's trying out her matchmaking skills again. Aunt Janice, who do you have in mind for our Riley? The science teacher? Annie wasn't interested in him; maybe Aunt Janice thinks he's the right one for you."

Riley looked at her aunt who was suddenly fussing over the coffee mugs. "Aunt Janice? Is it true?"

"Is what true, sweetie?" she asked, looking vague.

"You know exactly what I'm talking about!" Riley called out. "Let me spell it out for you again. I'm not in the market, nor will I ever be in the market, for a husband. You know what happened the one time I tried that. I'm single and very happy, thank you very much."

"Aunt Janice still denies getting me to visit her under false pretenses." Aiden chuckled.

"I asked you to do a story about Marietta's Valentine's

Day," their aunt said. "I didn't know you were going to hurt yourself in the airport, nor could I know you'd fall for Vivian the moment you saw her."

"It was also your idea to get Craig to help Annie with marketing her B and B," Aiden said.

Aunt Janice threw her hands up. "Yes, I asked him to help Annie. How could I know they already had feelings for one another?"

Laughing, Aiden hugged her. "You forget we know you too well. You can deny all you want to—we know it was all orchestrated by you."

"As long as you remember I'm not interested in a husband, I'm happy to visit you." Riley chuckled.

"What's a husband, Mommy?" Dylan asked.

Aware of all the eyes on her, Riley frantically searched for the right words. Her son was at the stage where he asked lots of questions, not all of them appropriate and not all of them in ideal situations. "Well, for instance, Uncle Craig is Aunt Annie's husband, and Uncle Aiden is Aunt Vivian's husband."

Frowning, Dylan stared at her. "'Cause we had weddings and they kissed?"

Everyone chuckled.

"Indeed," Riley said, meeting Mitch's eyes. "They got married, so now they are husbands and wives."

Dylan was still frowning, though, looking from her to Mitch. "Uncle Mitch doesn't yell anymore. He kissed you.

He'll be a nice husband."

Dropping her head in her palm, Riley shook her head while the others laughed. Dylan had the uncanny ability to connect dots at the most inopportune moments. "It doesn't work that way, sweetie. Do you want anything to eat?"

Fortunately, her son was still at the age where food trumped just about anything else, even talks about husbands.

Still chuckling, Aunt Janice took a plastic container out of the fridge. "I've made sandwiches. I thought Dylan might be hungry when you arrived."

Frowning, Aiden looked from Mitch to Riley. "So, why is this the first time I've heard Mitch kissed you?"

"Oh, come on, Aiden." Riley smiled, trying to make light of the whole situation. "We're practically family. He's kissed me good-bye, that's it."

"Well, I still vividly remember the hard time you gave me about Vivian, so I'm watching you," Aiden said to Mitch.

"What about more tea?" Aunt Janice asked.

Aiden gave her a hug. "Well, seeing that you're not seriously ill as you've had Riley believe, I'm off. Craig will probably also stop by. He was seeing a client when I called to tell him you're so ill Riley has dropped everything back in Portland and is on her way to visit." He kissed Riley on the forehead. "I'm glad you're here, sis. I hope we'll see you tonight?"

"What's happening tonight?" Riley asked.

Aiden smiled. "Small towns are busy over Christmas, I've discovered. By tonight, all the shops in town will have their Christmas decorations done, I'm told. Everybody in town gathers to walk down Main Street up to the courthouse for the lighting of the Christmas tree."

"Sounds fun, thanks. It would be lovely to see the family."

"Vivian has invited everyone for lunch on Sunday. I hope you'll be able to join us, as well?" Aiden continued. "She'd be so happy to know you're here. You can tell her all about kissing Mitch tonight."

"Seriously," Riley muttered, avoiding looking at Mitch.

Smiling, Aunt Janice took Aiden's arm. "Let me walk you out." She and Aiden disappeared down the corridor.

Dylan had discovered the small cars Aunt Janice kept in a basket in the kitchen and was happily playing, totally unaffected by the small bomb he'd dropped minutes ago.

Mitch was sipping his tea, his gaze on her. She'd forgotten the impact of the unusual combination of one blue and one brown eye.

"So, how have you been?" she asked.

"I'm well, thank you. What about you?"

"Great. I love the new job; it's just been crazy busy. You're writing a novel, I believe. How is that going?"

"I've just finished."

"That's great. And? Have you sent it to a publisher?"

He shook his head. "I'm not quite there yet. I've asked

my sisters to read it. I can trust them to be brutally honest. When I get their feedback, I'll start editing."

"If you're looking for more people to read your manuscript, I'm here for the next week. I won't hold my punches either."

"You never do." He grinned. "Thank you, I'll think about it."

For a moment, it was silent in the kitchen. From the direction of the front door, they could hear that Aunt Janice and Aiden were still talking.

Mitch cleared his throat. "You never responded to my text. Four months is a long time."

The front door closed. Aunt Janice was returning to the kitchen, thank goodness. "Oh, I responded. I just never sent it."

Mitch's eyes narrowed, but before he could reply, Aunt Janice was back. "Oh, sweetie, I'm so happy you're here. Please don't be angry with an old woman, but I've missed you so."

Smiling, Riley hugged her. "I've been so worried about you. I'm here for the week, but then we have to go back. I still have a few photo shoots until the week before Christmas. Fortunately, editing I can do from anywhere."

"I just hope you won't be working all day. I've spoken to Joanna who has the prekindergarten class, and she said Dylan is very welcome to join their group for the week."

"I don't like school," Dylan said, getting up from playing

with a nativity set.

"Have you made any friends?" Aunt Janice asked.

"Yeah. I like Luca and Sadie, but I don't like George. He says I shouldn't play with Sadie, 'cause she's a girl."

"I'm sure if he gets to know Sadie, he'll like her, too." Aunt Janice smiled. "Tell you what. I'll go with you on Monday, and if you don't like it, you don't have to go again. How does that sound?"

Dylan gave the idea some thought before he nodded. "Okay."

Mitch got up. "I have to go. I'll see you all later tonight?"

Aunt Janice clapped her hands. "Oh, I'm so happy to have all of you here. It just hasn't been the same without you, Riley. Would you mind seeing Mitch off? I want to start dinner. We can have a quick bite before we leave for the Christmas Stroll." Still muttering, she turned away and opened the fridge.

"I'm sure Mitch can walk to the front door all by himself," Riley said coolly.

"Manners, Riley, dear. Manners," Aunt Janice said, her back still to them.

Mitch's eyes were filled with laughter. "Yes, Riley, manners."

"Seriously," she muttered as she marched to the front door. Opening the door, she waited for Mitch to leave.

He took her hand, though, pulling her outside with him.

"Mitch, what—" But that was as far as she got.

He swooped down. She just had time to see his eyes darken before his mouth closed around hers. His lips were urgent, hot, and on a mission. Within seconds, she was shivering, burning up. Her hands reached out, and grabbing his shirt, she pulled him closer.

Just when she was about to go up in flames, Mitch lifted his head. His breathing was ragged, his eyes mere slits. "It's all I've been thinking about for four months."

Gulping in some much-needed oxygen, Riley dropped her hands. Before she could respond to his words, though, she noticed Mitch's rumpled shirt. "Sorry about this." Muttering, she tried to iron out the material. With her hands.

Inhaling sharply, Mitch took her hand in his. "You touching me is not helping," he growled. "We have to talk."

Riley groaned softly. "About what? This is crazy. You can't just kiss me whenever you want."

"So what do I have to do to be able to do that?"

"What do you mean?"

"What do I have to do to be able to kiss you whenever I want?"

Her breath lodged somewhere in her throat. Gulping in some fresh air, she frantically tried to find the right words. "Mitch, seriously, you know this whole whatever it is, is ridiculous. We're practically family…"

One big, warm hand cupped her face. "We're not related. Please don't try and hide behind that."

"So, what do you want? Make out and kiss around corners?"

He grinned, his thumb caressing her face. "I won't mind doing that, but I want much more."

"Like what?"

"It's very simple, Riley. What I want is you." The look in his eyes was threatening to rekindle the slow-burning embers of desire.

She gave a step back. "The whole thing is way too complicated. I think it's best to just stop right here. I have a son; I can't just think about what I want and have a quick fling. My life, my job, my house are in Portland."

Chapter Six

MITCH HAD HIS next argument ready, but before he could say anything, there was a movement behind them.

"So what's going on here?" a voice asked. Damn. It was Craig, Riley's cousin.

Mitch dropped his hand and turned around to face him. "Hi, Craig."

Craig was frowning. "Why do you have your hands all over my cousin?"

Riley sighed. "Oh, come on, Craig. Mitch was just leaving. We're…"

Mitch quickly looked at Riley. If she told one more person they were related, he wouldn't be responsible for his actions.

Catching his eye, Riley grimaced. "Mitch was telling me about the Christmas Stroll. Are you and Annie also going?"

But Craig was not letting this go. "So, why is he touching you?"

"He was saying good-bye. That's it. Come say hi to Dylan; he's missed you."

"Remember the hard time you gave me about Annie? I'm watching you." With another fierce glance in his direction, Craig stomped past Mitch into the house.

"See what you've done?" Riley whispered. "The last thing I need is my brother and cousin on my back about you. Let's just forget about this."

Mitch put his hands in his pockets; he didn't trust they wouldn't reach out to Riley again without any message from his brain. "It's been four months, Riley. I haven't been able to forget a single thing about you."

She caught her breath, her eyes darkened. He waited.

"Nothing can come of it, Mitch, you know that. Having been jilted at the altar has cured me of ever going down the relationship and marriage road again. I also have a son to think of."

"So, what? I'm just supposed to forget what has happened between us?"

"People kiss all the—"

Before she could finish her sentence, he pulled her closer and kissed her again. Only when she melted against him, her body pliant and shivering, did he lift his head.

"Not like this they don't," he growled before he turned away and walked toward his car.

What the hell was he doing? He had no business lusting after Riley O'Sullivan of all people. His two sisters were married to Riley's brother and cousin. It made the whole thing even more complicated.

She was right—this should end right here.

He glanced back toward the front door. Riley was still standing there, her fingers on her lips—how was he supposed to forget this picture?

Cussing, he stepped on the gas. What happened between him and Riley when they were together wasn't that easy to ignore. What was more—he wasn't the only one who thought so.

<hr />

RILEY'S INSIDES WERE still shivering by the time Aunt Janice stopped on Main Street, and it wasn't from the cold. What Mitch's kisses did to her…

"Ooh, Mommy, look at all the Christmas lights!" Dylan called out.

Blinking, Riley tried to focus on what was going on around her. The previous times she'd been in Marietta, she'd been fascinated by the beautiful Old West ambience of the town. With classic western storefronts, the magnificent mountains surrounding it, Marietta was indeed a beautiful place.

And now, for Christmas, the town had been transformed into a winter wonderland. Every single store along the street was lit up by Christmas lights and decorations.

"Come on, you two," Aunt Janice called out as she got out of the car. "The parade is about to start. There's Annie and Vivian!"

Riley made sure Dylan's jacket was buttoned up; he had his gloves on, and his knitted ear-flap hat was covering his ears. As she got out of the car, she gasped. "Wow, it's cold!" She crouched down and helped her son out of the car. "Come on, sweetie, let's go say hi to Aunt Annie and Aunt Vivian."

Dylan looked wide-eyed at everything around them. "So many lights," he breathed, apparently not even aware of the cold.

"Aunt Janice, Riley!" called Annie as she and Vivian hurried over to meet them.

Smiling broadly, Annie hugged Riley. "I'm so, so happy you're here!" she called out before she bent down to pick up Dylan. She kissed him on the cheeks until he laughed before she put him down again.

Chuckling, Vivian also hugged Riley. "I believe we have a lot of catching up to do."

"Ask her about kissing Mitch," Aiden said as he and Craig also reached them.

Ignoring her brother's words, Riley looked around them. "Any place close-by where we can get something hot to drink? It's freezing!"

"Sage Carrigan's chocolate shop is just ahead," Vivian said, pointing down the road. "You haven't tasted chocolate until you've tasted her hot chocolate."

"Oh, look, here's the parade!" Aunt Janice's voice was

nearly drowned by the noise.

Dylan tugged at Riley's jeans. "Can't see, Mommy."

Riley picked up her son. One of these days he was going to be too big, but for now, she loved that he still wanted her to pick him up.

"Horses, Mommy, look!" he called out, his eyes bright with joy.

Hugging him close, they watched as the parade of horses and carts, a fire truck, a big truck with a waving, smiling Santa, passed down Main Street.

It looked as if the whole town of Marietta had gathered on the sidewalks to cheer on the parade. As far as the eye could see, the street was lined with cheering, happy people as the parade moved along the street.

"Come on, guys, I seriously need that hot chocolate now," Craig said. "I'm still not used to this cold."

"But I want to talk to Santa," Dylan said.

Annie smiled at him. "You will, don't worry. At the end of the street is the courthouse, and everybody meets there to light the big Christmas tree. Santa will be there."

"Really?" Dylan asked, his eyes wide with wonder.

"Yes, come on, I can smell the hot chocolate already!" Annie said.

Riley touched Annie's arm. "I was finally working on your wedding photos when Aunt Janice called. But I promise to finish them before I leave."

Annie beamed. "Oohh, I can't wait. We've, of course,

seen photos other people took on their phones, but I'm so excited to see yours. May I come and look at what you have?"

"I still have to edit…"

"I know, I know, but just a sneak peek?"

Riley laughed. "Of course. What about tomorrow morning?"

"Great. I have guests, but after their breakfast I'm free. What about lunch?"

"Won't you be tired?" Riley asked.

Craig hugged his wife. "Cooking makes her happy. I'm also looking forward to seeing your photos. Aunt Janice? I hope you'll also join us?"

But Riley wasn't listening anymore. Her heart had skidded to a stop. Mitch was standing in front of the chocolate shop talking to a pretty blonde who had her hands on his arms.

"What is Mitch doing with Sandra?" Annie muttered.

"Is that Sandra who has the new deli in town?" Aunt Janice asked.

"Yep," Annie said. "She'd set her sights on Craig before and now it seems on Mitch."

"I thought Mitch was kissing Riley," Aiden added.

They were nearly on top of the couple who were standing in front of the chocolate shop.

"Hi, Mitch," Vivian called out.

Mitch looked up, his eyes zooming in on Riley. A smiling Sandra turned around to face them, her hands still clutching Mitch's arm.

Her heart breaking into little pieces, Riley nodded in their direction before she made her way into the shop, Dylan still on her arm.

"Who is that lady, Mommy?" Dylan asked.

"I don't know, sweetie. What about a hot chocolate? With marshmallows?"

A slim redhead smiled at her from behind the counter. "Hi, I'm Sage. You're Aiden's sister and Craig's cousin if I'm not mistaken." She smiled, motioning toward Riley's hair.

"Yes, I am. Riley, pleased to meet another redhead. We've heard about your hot chocolate and must try it, I believe," Riley said. "Two, please, with marshmallows."

"Hi, Sage," a voice said behind them.

Her heart sank. Mitch. Riley tried to ignore him, but Mitch touched her arm.

"Hi. Let me take Dylan."

Before she could protest, Dylan was in Mitch's arms.

"One for me, too, please, Sage," he said.

At the same time, Annie, Craig, Vivian, Aiden, and Aunt Janice also entered the small shop, rubbing hands and calling out for hot chocolate.

Mitch put a hand to Riley's back, moving them to the side.

"Is your lady friend not waiting for you?" Riley asked below her breath.

"The only lady friend I want to be with is right next to me."

"She looked right at home with her hands all over you." The words slipped out before Riley could stop herself.

Fortunately, Sage called out her name. Saved by hot chocolate, thank goodness.

Mitch had Dylan in his arms, though, so she had to wait for him to get his own hot chocolate before they could leave.

"We'll see you at the tree," Mitch said before he followed her outside.

As they stepped outside, Sandra was hovering at the entrance, her eyes brightening as she saw Mitch.

Riley turned to Mitch. "You can put Dylan down, thank you. It would be easier while he's drinking his hot chocolate. Then you can join your lady friend. We'll wait for the others."

The moment Mitch put Dylan down, Sandra grabbed his arm. "Mitch! There you are. I…"

Blindly, Riley took Dylan by the hand and, turning away, followed the other strollers down the street. Something had tightened around her chest, making it difficult to breathe. Fortunately, Dylan was unaware of her near panic and kept on chattering.

This was exactly what she'd wanted; she should be glad Mitch had found someone else. Only hours earlier, she'd told him in so many words that there couldn't be anything between them.

So, why was she upset? Why was the sight of Mitch with someone else stealing her breath?

"Here you are," Aiden said before he slipped an arm around her. "I know Aunt Janice has conned you into visiting, but we're all so happy to see you."

She leaned into his warmth for a moment. "It's lovely to be here."

"Where's Mitch?"

"I don't know. I caught a few of your articles in the newspaper in Portland. How do you like working from here?"

"Mmm, you're changing the subject. Okay, but at some point I want to know what's going on between you and Mitch."

"Not a thing. He's with Sandy or Sandra or whatever her name is. You've seen them. What else are you doing besides writing for the newspaper?"

With another long look in her direction, Aiden began to talk about his work. Riley smiled and nodded, but she had no idea what her brother was saying. She wanted to turn around, grab Mitch by the hand, and pull him away from the other woman.

She was jealous. She'd never been jealous before. Not a nice feeling.

Cussing softly, Mitch made his way down Main Street to the courthouse. Where the hell was Riley? He'd turned his head toward Sandra for a moment, and when he looked back, the crowd had swallowed up both Riley and Dylan.

Sandra was nice and pretty, but she wasn't the one he wanted to be with, damn it. Surely Riley knew that.

His eyes scanned the crowd gathered in front of the big conifer tree. There she was. Aiden was standing next to her with Dylan in his arms. With long strides, Mitch made his way toward them.

Riley was smiling at something Annie was saying to her, but when she saw him approaching, her smile slipped. With another step, he reached her.

"I was looking for you," he said as he took her hand.

She tried to pull her hand out of his, but he laced their fingers.

"So where's Sandra, Mitch?" Vivian chuckled. "She seems to be a very… uh… tactile person."

"Not sure," Mitch said, ignoring his sister's gaze on his hand around Riley's.

"The way she was touching you, I thought she's your date," Annie added.

"No, she's not. I don't know—"

A commotion to the side drew his attention. Damn it, not again.

"Excuse me." Dropping Riley's hand, Mitch hurried over to where Patrick Thomas was staggering around, swearing at everyone around him.

"Mr. Thomas," he greeted the drunken man. "How are you doing? Where's Matthew?"

Patrick glared at him through bloodshot eyes, swaying from side to side. "That useless son of mine? I whipped his ass, I did. You're the one who put ideas into his head. It's on you if he's hurt!" The next moment, he crashed down, beer bottle still in his hand.

Gnashing his teeth together, Mitch bent down to help Patrick up, but he was out cold.

"It's okay, Mitch, I've got it from here." One of the deputy sheriffs of Marietta stepped closer.

"I'll go and check up on Matthew," Mitch said.

"That poor boy. He's got another year of school, but Patrick isn't making it easy on him. When his wife died, he just fell apart," the deputy sheriff said.

"No excuse to use his son for a punching bag," Mitch growled, his hands in fists.

"While Matthew keeps denying it, there's nothing we can do. Let me know how he's doing, please."

Mitch turned away, seeing red. He was so angry, but being angry at a drunk was a useless exercise, he knew. Matthew Thomas was in one of his classes. He didn't have to be a psychologist to know the boy was always looking for trouble because he was having a hard time at home.

Mitch hated bullies, maybe because he'd been a target while at school. At least he'd had his parents who'd always had his back. Once they'd realized what had been going on, they'd made an appointment to see his teachers. Matthew didn't have anyone looking out for him. The person who was responsible for his safety was the one who was hurting him.

"Mitch? Everything okay?"

He looked up to see Riley had followed him. Taking her hand, he drew her away from the scene. She would've seen what had happened; he didn't have to explain. "It's the dad of one of my students. I have to go and see if Matthew is okay."

"Of course, you don't have to explain." She began to pull her hand from his but held on for a moment longer.

"I'm only here tonight because I knew you'd be here."

"Mitch…"

"Still want to forget about what's going on between us?"

"It's the best thing to do. We should go back to just being friends."

Nodding, he dropped her hand. "If that's what you want. I'll see you, friend." Turning on his heel, he jogged to his car.

She was right. The whole thing was ridiculous. So why the hell was there a hole where his heart was supposed to be?

Chapter Seven

WITH EVERY STEP Riley walked away from Mitch, more pieces of her heart fell to the ground. She was doing the right thing, damn it. So why did it feel so wrong? She'd always relied on her gut to tell her what was right and what was wrong, but being jilted by someone she'd trusted had changed that. She'd realized she couldn't always trust her instinct.

She was doing the only logical thing—walking away from Mitch. But damn it, it hurt.

As she reached her family, they were still talking about the unfortunate incident.

"My heart goes out to Matthew," Aunt Janice was saying. "He has always been one of those model students, getting good grades, but then his mom died about a year ago, the dad started drinking, and since then, his life hasn't been easy. Mitch is doing so much to help him, though, but it's tough with a dad like his."

"Mitch has told us about Matthew," Annie said. "I'm so sorry for the boy."

"Mitch is really trying to help him…" Vivian began just

as her phone rang. "It's Mitch," she said frowning and walked away to talk.

Riley crossed her arms, trying to focus on her breathing. What was happening here had nothing to do with her. She and Dylan were leaving in a few days; she was doing the right thing stopping things between her and Mitch before it became even more complicated.

Vivian put her phone away. "That was Mitch. Matthew is badly hurt, and Mitch is taking him to the hospital. I have to go." She looked at Aiden. "You can go back with Annie and Craig?"

"I'll take you," Aiden said and took her arm.

"It may take a while," she said.

Aiden hugged her. "It won't be the first time I have to wait for you."

Dylan tugged at Riley's jeans. "Mom, can we go see Santa?"

Blinking, she focused on her son. "Of course, sweetie. Let's see where he is."

RILEY HAD THOUGHT Dylan would fall asleep on their way home. It had been a long day, but he was so excited about everything he'd seen, he hadn't stopped talking since they'd left Main Street.

"So what did you tell Santa you want for Christmas?"

Aunt Janice asked Dylan as they entered her house.

"It's a secret." Dylan smiled.

"Surely, you can tell me?" Aunt Janice teased as she closed the door behind them.

Dylan looked at Riley. "Okay, but you can't tell Mommy."

"Why?" Riley asked, feigning to be indignant.

"The secret's about you," Dylan explained.

Aunt Janice bent down. "I won't tell."

As Dylan whispered in Aunt Janice's ear, her eyes widened. "Well," she said, avoiding Riley's eyes as she stood up straight, "you never know. We may just get a Christmas miracle."

Dylan's eyes were round. "What's a Christmas miracle?"

"When wishes come true." Aunt Janice grinned. "It's been a long day for you two. Anything else you need?"

Dylan yawned.

Smiling, Riley took his hand. "Someone is finally a bit tired."

"While you put him in bed, I'll make tea," Aunt Janice said.

Swallowing a groan, Riley nodded. She knew exactly what *I'll make tea* meant. Aunt Janice had questions.

Fifteen minutes later, Riley was back in the kitchen.

"Dylan asleep?" Aunt Janice asked as she poured the tea.

"Out like a light."

"Great, come and sit. We have to talk."

Riley pulled out a chair. "What about?"

"You know what about. You and Mitch. Everyone around you can feel the sparks when the two of you are in the same room."

"I told you I'm not interested in relationships."

"Oh, that's nonsense. You never really loved Percy, and if you're very honest, you'd agree. Everyone around you was getting married, and you went along with the tide."

"You never liked him, did you?"

"His eyes are close-set, a clear sign of someone with a weak will."

Riley's eyebrows shot up. "How do you know that?"

"I don't need to study physio… What do you call it again?"

"Are you talking about physiognomy?" Riley chuckled.

"I remember you were into it a while ago. I know nothing about the subject, trust me, but he never treated you right, long before he'd sent you that horrible text on your wedding day. But you can't let one guy steal your joy forever. Don't push someone like Mitch away because you've been hurt once. Getting hurt is part of life. But in between the hardships, there is so much love. You just have to open your heart to it."

"Yeah?" Riley asked. "You're happily single, aren't you?"

"I am, but it's not by choice. Don't make the same mistake I did. I thought there was time. We were young; I had places to go, things to see. Let's wait, I said. Turned out, time was the one thing we didn't have, that my Grant didn't have. He died of cancer. Within a month."

Riley reached out to touch her aunt's hand. "I'm so sorry to hear that. Why haven't you told me before? Do Craig and Aiden know?"

Aunt Janice nodded. "Both of them needed a bit of a nudge. You've been so strong, making a home for you and Dylan, and I know it's scary to think you may lose everything you've worked so hard for, but sweetie, love is worth the risk, trust me. You're afraid of commitment and I don't blame you, but at some point you have to give yourself permission to go out and experience life again. Falling in love with the right person doesn't mean you have to lose your identity or your security. Trusting anyone after what happened to you is a huge step, I know, but you need to do that if you want to grow. Okay, there, I'm finished." She grinned.

Long after Aunt Janice had gone to bed, Riley was still sitting in the kitchen, mulling over her aunt's words. Yes, she'd been afraid of getting hurt, and she was scared of trusting anyone else, but she had Dylan to think about, as well. She couldn't simply fall for the first guy who kissed her senseless.

Involuntary, her fingers touched her lips again. What Mitch's kisses did to her...

Groaning, she got up, cleaned the cups, switched off the lights. From outside, the Christmas lights still lit up the whole house. Every surface in the house was covered with one or other Christmas decoration. She tiptoed into Dylan's room. He was out for the count. As she pulled up the blankets, she thought of Mitch tenderly doing the same thing four months ago.

She'd been a bit wary of him since the first day she'd met him. He'd been scowling and yelling at Aiden. She'd labeled him the yelling brother and hadn't given him another thought.

But then she'd danced with him, kissed him, and… well, everything was different now.

He was one of the good guys. Tonight, she'd been witness to his caring nature, his compassion for one of his students. Even the way he'd handled the drunken dad was impressive. A teddy bear, his sisters called him—now she knew why.

Mitch. Always Mitch. What was she going to do about him? He'd agreed to being just friends, but was friendship really all she wanted from him?

Being just friends would mean they'd see one another but not touch or kiss. Never kiss Mitch again?

Groaning, she walked to her room. She was going to bed now; she was so tired, she couldn't see straight. Maybe her subconscious would miraculously come up with a plan so that she would know what to do about Mitch.

BY THE TIME Mitch got home, it was after midnight. Tired and upset, he switched off the lights and went to his room.

He'd been trying to help Matthew since he'd become aware of the boy's circumstances at home, but Matthew kept telling him everything was okay—that he'd fallen from his bike or walked into a door—he'd always had an excuse. Tonight was the first time the boy had asked for help.

After Mitch had left the hospital, he'd phoned the principal at the high school. They'd spoken about Matthew before, and after tonight's incident, she'd get in touch with the maternal grandparents who apparently lived in Butte.

What Matthew needed was love and a stable home. Mitch inhaled deeply. Not everyone was lucky enough to have parents like he and Vivian and Annie had had.

Children. Marriage. The whole happily-ever-after thing had never even crossed his mind. It would happen someday, he'd always thought. Back in Sacramento, there simply hadn't been time for anything except work.

Besides, although he had two sisters, he'd always been slightly awkward when dealing with the opposite sex. It wasn't easy these days to know what was the right thing to do. His dad had taught him to open doors for women, to stand up when they entered a room, to treat them with respect, but he'd discovered the few times he'd dated a woman, things had obviously changed, and that not all women welcomed these gestures. Women nowadays insisted on opening their own doors. He didn't have a problem with that; he was just never sure when to do what. Not bothering to date had been his solution to the problem.

Anyway, since he and his sisters had moved to Marietta, his main concern was to make sure they were happy. Dating anyone had been the last thing on his mind. Although Vivian and Annie were now married, both obviously in love with their husbands, he'd always feel responsible for them. But living close to them, he could pop in at any time to make sure they were okay. Teaching kept him busy, and life was uneventful. He was content. Okay, maybe not deliriously happy, but who was?

Four months ago, at Craig and Annie's wedding, his whole world had been turned upside down, though. He'd danced with Riley; he'd held her in his arms, kissed her. She challenged him, made him laugh, made him ache. He'd discovered he liked being with her. He liked the person he was when he was with her.

But it wasn't what she wanted. She wanted to be friends. It shouldn't bother him. It wasn't as if he wanted to be responsible for one more person's happiness.

Deep in thought, he took out his phone. It had vibrated a few times while he'd been at the hospital. It was a message from Annie. Aunt Janice, Riley, and Dylan were coming to lunch, and he was welcome to join them.

His heart missed a beat. Riley would also be there.

Grimacing, he walked to the bathroom. There was no way he could only be friends with Riley. What was more, she felt the same way. He'd kissed her, he knew.

Chapter Eight

R ILEY AND ANNIE had just sat down at the kitchen table to look at the wedding photos on Riley's laptop, Aunt Janice watching over their shoulders, when the doorbell rang.

"It's either Vivian and Craig or Mitch," Annie said as she jumped up.

Riley closed her eyes. She probably should've guessed Annie would also invite the rest of the fam, but she wasn't quite prepared to see Mitch again so soon.

"You okay?" Aunt Janice asked.

"Yes, I'm just admiring Annie's Christmas decorations," Riley improvised. "You've always made a big deal out of Christmas, and your house is beautifully decorated, but this…"

Aunt Janice laughed. "Annie takes Christmas to a whole new level, for sure."

"Everyone has arrived!" Annie announced merrily as she returned to the kitchen.

Riley got up from her chair to greet the family. Vivian and Aiden entered first, and right behind them, looking seriously sexy in a blue denim shirt and black pants, was a smiling Mitch. Her heart skidded to a stop. Damn, the man just did something to her.

His eyes met hers briefly before he crouched down in front of Dylan. "Hey, you."

To Riley's surprise, Dylan threw his arms around Mitch's shoulders and hugged him. "Hello, Uncle Mitch."

Mitch met her gaze, his eyes strangely bright. "Now, that's a nice way to be greeted. Hello, Dylan. Did you enjoy the Christmas Stroll?"

Dylan nodded. "I talked to Santa."

"Did you tell him what you want for Christmas?" Vivian asked, ruffling his hair.

"Yes, but it's a secret," Dylan whispered.

"Not even I know." Riley chuckled as Vivian hugged her. "He's told Aunt Janice, though."

"Well, if Aunt Janice knows, maybe your wish will come true." Craig grinned.

"The food is ready, but I want to look at the wedding photos," Annie said. "Who wants to join us?" Everyone's hand went up.

"Oh, my goodness, guys." Riley tried to stop the enthusiasm. "I haven't finished editing the photos. I was only going to show it to Annie."

Aiden smiled. "Sorry, sis—you're here, we're here, your laptop is here, let's do this. But the screen of your laptop is way too small—let's connect it to the television screen. It would be like watching a movie."

Minutes later, they were all gathered around the television in the living room. While everyone else found a chair, Riley sat down on the floor next to Dylan.

"I'll bring another chair, sis," Aiden said.

Riley shook her head. "I'm totally fine here; this way, I'm close to my laptop."

She didn't see where Mitch was sitting, but if the heat radiating against her back was any indication, he was directly behind her.

Friends. They were just friends. This was good. This was what she wanted.

"Okay, here we go!" she called out and clicked on the first photo.

Amongst *aaahs* and *ooohs* and laughter and sniffling, they went through all the photos of the day.

"Oh, Riley," Annie cried toward the end. "Go back to the previous one."

"This one?" Riley smiled. It was the one where Craig had touched his bride's face in an unguarded moment.

"Look at that face!" Aiden chuckled. "Coz, you're clearly besotted." Aiden chuckled.

Craig hugged Annie. "What can I say? I married the love of my life."

"This one—I want this enlarged and framed, Riley, please?" Annie asked.

"On canvas?" Riley nodded as she showed the last two photos. "I can have it done for you when we're back in

Portland. I don't know when you guys will be visiting again?" Closing the folder with wedding photos, she turned around to look at Annie and Aiden, trying her best not to look in Mitch's direction.

"I know you have to go back for more photo shoots," Aiden said with a frown. "But aren't you coming back for Christmas?"

"I don't know…" Riley began, but that was as far as she got.

"You can't not be here," Vivian called out. "It's our first Christmas as a family and you should be here—with family."

"We'll buy the plane tickets if money is a problem," Aiden added.

"It's not the plane tickets…" Riley tried.

"Then it's settled," Aiden said. "You're coming back for Christmas."

"And maybe, if Dylan likes the school here, he could stay with me for the two weeks you have to go back to Portland," Aunt Janice said.

Laughing, Riley threw up her hands. "Okay, I'll think about it."

Annie jumped up and gave Riley a hug. "We'll pester you until you say yes. Let's eat. Aiden—will you open the wine?"

As everyone left, Riley turned back to pick up her laptop. She knelt down to close it and put it in the bag, but before she even touched her laptop, Mitch crouched down beside her.

"I can see why you're such a successful photographer—the pictures you've taken are really something else." He pulled the laptop closer to him. "I want to have another look... which folder?"

Frozen, Riley saw Mitch's finger hovering over the folder she'd created for his photos.

"This is an interesting name for a folder. SOMETHING STUPID," he said.

Finally, Riley got her breath back. Just before Mitch could click on the folder, she grabbed her laptop. "It's a good description for what's in it." Jumping up, she closed it and put it in the cover.

"So what have you got hidden in there?" Mitch chuckled.

She tried to shrug nonchalant. "Exactly what it says. Stupid moments. When doing fashion shoots, there are a lot of those."

"Mitch? Riley?" Annie called from inside.

"Coming!" Riley called, turning away from Mitch. As she entered the dining room, she put her laptop down on one of the smaller tables near the wall. She'd be able to keep an eye on it while eating.

She should've deleted the photos of Mitch. What had she been thinking? She hadn't been thinking, that was what.

Everyone was already sitting down around the table, the only two open chairs next to one another. Swallowing her groan, Riley put on a smile and sat down.

Mitch pulled out the other chair and sat down next to her. Within seconds, his heat, his scent was seeping into her pores. If she didn't burst into flames soon, it would be a miracle. A hysterical giggle threatened to erupt. Who had mentioned Christmas miracles?

WITH THE SMELL of orange blossoms making him lightheaded, Mitch tried to focus on the conversation around him. After a while, he gave up; there was such a roaring in his ears, he was only able to pick up a word here and there.

Restlessly, he shifted on his chair. Under the big, white tablecloth, his leg touched Riley's. She tried to move, but there wasn't anywhere to go. Fidgeting, she let her hands slip from her lap to the chair and back. Clenching his teeth, he reached for her hand under the tablecloth. For a moment, it fluttered like a scared bird before it stilled.

The roaring quieted, his heart settled. He was finally able to touch her.

"Mitch, do you know how Matthew is doing?" Janice interrupted his thoughts.

"I visited him this morning; he'll be okay physically. Mentally, I'm not so sure."

"The poor kid," Janice said, her eyes bright with tears. "Ever since his mom died, he's had a rough road."

"I saw him just before lunch," Vivian said. "The principal from school was there, and we spoke a few words. She'd contacted the grandparents, and they're on their way. Apparently, after their daughter's passing, their son-in-law didn't want to see them or have them contact Matthew, so they had no idea what was going on."

Mitch looked at his watch. "Do you know what time they'll be arriving?"

"They were going to leave as soon as possible. It's a nearly two-hour drive, so you can finish your lunch."

"I want to speak to them and make sure he's okay."

Under the table, Riley pressed his hand. A small gesture, but he felt ten feet tall.

As Mitch picked up his fork, he noticed Vivian was whispering something in her husband's ear, but Aiden just smiled and shook his head before he softly spoke to her. What would that be all about?

Mitch quickly finished his meal. He was being rude, but this might be the only chance he had to talk to Matthew's grandparents. "If you'll excuse me?"

"Of course," Annie said, getting up. "We'll have dessert when you're back."

Nodding, he got up. "I shouldn't be long." As he turned around, he touched Riley's shoulder. He hadn't even thought about what he was doing—wanting to touch her was instinctive.

When exactly this need to put his hands on her had

started, he wasn't sure. What he did know was that it wasn't something that was going to change anytime soon.

———

ANNIE HAD INSISTED on looking at the wedding photos again. Riley had fetched the laptop, and while she and Annie, with Aunt Janice and Vivian behind them, scrolled through the photos again, Craig and Aiden were chatting. Dylan was playing with his cars.

Riley was trying to go through the photos as quickly as she could. Nobody knew exactly when Mitch would return, but she wanted her laptop closed and in its bag when he did.

They were nearly done when Dylan ran up to her. "I'm thirsty, Mommy."

Reluctantly, Riley got up. She should never have left the folder on her computer.

As she took Dylan's hand, Mitch walked back into the dining room. His eyes met hers before he saw the women looking at the photos again.

"Hi, everyone," he greeted. "Are we looking at the photos again?"

"I can't get enough." Annie smiled as she moved to sit down on the chair where Riley had sat. "I can understand why you're such a sought-after photographer, Riley. These are really something. Mitch, look, I love this one of you. Riley somehow captured exactly who you are—your goofy smile, your caring nature—this one is my favorite of you, I think."

"Didn't you say we can have dessert once Mitch is back?" Aiden asked. "What can I do?"

Smiling, Annie got up. "Let's have dessert!"

Riley watched anxiously as Vivian leaned forward and pressed a few keys.

"Folder closed, Riley. Annie? What can I do to help?"

Aunt Janice also turned away to help Annie while Craig and Aiden moved closer to Mitch.

"Mommy," Dylan mumbled.

"Let's get you some water," Riley said. Her cousin and brother and Mitch were deep in conversation; surely nobody would open the folder on her laptop while she was gone? With a last glance in their direction, she took Dylan to the kitchen.

Chapter Nine

WHILE CRAIG AND Aiden were talking, he noticed Janice approaching Riley's laptop again.

She winked as she caught his eye. "I'm a sucker for weddings. I just have to look at these gorgeous ones again. Beautiful reminders of a special day. Mitch, do you know where to look?"

Shaking his head, Mitch walked over to her. "Let me see…"

But one of Janice's fingers was already pressing down on a button. "Oh, look, Mitch, there are more photos of you here."

"Aunt Janice!" Vivian called from the kitchen. "We need your opinion on something."

"Excuse me, dear." Janice winked as she walked away.

Mitch barely heard her. His eyes were on the photograph on the laptop. It was of him but not one he'd seen before.

He clicked on the next one and the next. What the— Every single picture was of him. Annie was in one or two, Dylan in quite a few, but he was the focus in every single picture. And there were many. Closing the folder, he saw the name. SOMETHING STUPID. So photos of him were the something stupid?

"Still looking at wedding pictures?" Janice teased as she came back from the kitchen.

Quickly, he closed the laptop. "Riley did a great job, don't you think?"

"That she did. Which ones were you looking at? Show me?"

"Well…" he began not quite sure what to say, but fortunately Annie called them back to the table for dessert at that moment.

Janice cocked her head as she looked at Mitch. "What I would like to know, though, is which photo has put that stunned smile on your face."

She didn't wait for him to answer, but with a definite glint in her eye, turned around and joined the rest of the family at the table.

Could she have known about the photos? Nah, he didn't think so, although… Shaking his head he joined the rest of the family around the table.

He wouldn't put anything beyond Janice.

―――

RILEY WATCHED AS Dylan drank a glass of water. Only then he was happy to be put down.

"Riley, Dylan!" Vivian called before she appeared in the

kitchen door. "It's time for dessert. Come on." Taking Dylan's hand, she looked at Riley. "Everything okay? You look… rattled."

Riley smiled. "Everything is fine. Dylan was thirsty."

As they entered the dining room, Riley searched for Mitch. He was still standing in front of her computer. Their eyes met.

She didn't have to ask—the look in his eye confirmed her worst fears—he'd seen the photos. It wasn't quite clear how he'd discovered it, but he'd seen it.

Everyone else was already sitting around the table.

Before she could move closer to talk to Mitch, though, Aiden got up from his chair at the table and called everyone's attention.

"Riley, Mitch, come on, sit down. We have news." Smiling broadly, he took Vivian's hand in his. "We were going to tell you tomorrow, but then Riley arrived, and Annie invited everyone for lunch, and well…"

"We're pregnant!" Vivian called out.

"And my wife stole my moment." Aiden chuckled, bending down to kiss his wife.

For a moment there was a stunned silence.

Aunt Janice burst into tears. "I'm so happy!" She sniffled before jumping up to congratulate them.

It took a beat longer for Riley to grasp what her brother and his wife had said. She met Aiden's bright eyes. Wiping her own wet ones, she rushed to the happy couple. "So happy for you!"

While everyone was congratulating the couple, Craig brought a bottle of bubbly and glasses. "Vivian can't have any, but I'm quite happy to have an extra glass for the team." He grinned.

Still dazed, Riley went back to her chair. Her brother had always been so adamant he was never going to marry, but during a visit to Marietta, he'd met the lovely doctor in the ER, and now look at him. He was married to Vivian, he was obviously very happy, and they were going to have a baby.

Dylan tugged at her sleeve. "What's pregnant, Mommy?"

Everyone chuckled, waiting for Riley to explain. "It means Uncle Aiden and Aunt Vivian are going to have a baby," Riley said. She'd learned a while ago never to go into too much detail.

Dylan's eyes widened, and he looked at the two. "'Cause they kissed and had a wedding and Uncle Aiden is her husband?"

"He asked about husbands earlier today," Aunt Janice told everyone. "Made an interesting observation, too."

"Yes," Riley told Dylan. "And because they love each other."

The little boy's gaze went to Craig and Annie. "So, are Uncle Craig and Aunt Annie also having a baby?"

Annie laughed. "Not yet, Dylan, but one of these days, we hope."

Dylan's gaze landed on Riley. "So, Mommy, if Uncle

Mitch is your…"

"Dylan, no!" Riley called out just in time to stop her son from saying something that was bound to make an awkward situation even more awkward. Jumping up, she took Dylan's hand. "Come on, let me get you some more juice."

Quite a few chuckles followed Riley and Dylan as she quickly made her way to the kitchen.

"Are you mad at me?" Dylan asked, his bottom lip quivering.

"No, sweetie, it's just…" How did she explain to her four-year-old he shouldn't be talking about husbands in front of Mitch of all people?

"So, can I ask Uncle Mitch if he will be your husband?"

Groaning, Riley crouched down in front of her son. "Please don't talk about husbands, okay?"

Dylan stared at her with big, blue eyes. "But if you don't get a husband, we can't get a baby."

Her little boy was way too perceptive and quick to draw conclusions. "You and I are very happy by ourselves; we don't need anyone else. What about that juice?"

"'Kay," Dylan said, his shoulders slumping.

As she got up, a movement at the door made her look in that direction. Her eyes met Mitch's. He was leaning against one of the kitchen cupboards, watching them. Probably heard everything.

"You also want juice?" she asked as she poured some for Dylan.

"I'm fine, thanks."

Dylan took a few sips from the cup before he put the glass down. "Thank you, Mommy." Husbands fortunately forgotten for the moment, he ran back to the dining room.

"He's very intelligent, isn't he?" Mitch chuckled. "He was quick to make the connection between husbands and babies."

"He'll find out soon enough it doesn't always work like that. The way he's asking questions, he and I probably need to have the conversation about his daddy pretty soon."

"So, is Dylan's dad not in the picture at all?"

"No. His choice."

"You're an amazing mom. I hope you know that."

"We're doing okay."

Mitch moved closer. "The folder, something stupid…"

"You snooped."

"I didn't. Janice opened it."

"You shouldn't have looked."

"Every photo is of me."

"I… I know! I don't know how that happened."

"Because I kissed you."

"Most of those were taken before we danced and kissed and… I don't know how to explain it! Before the dance, I hadn't even thought… or I didn't know I was thinking…" She quickly swallowed the rest of her words. "Please just forget what you saw." Brushing past him, she made her way to the dining room to join the others. How did she explain something she didn't understand herself?

GNASHING HIS TEETH, Mitch crossed his arms as he stared at Riley's retreating back. The woman was driving him nuts. Forget about the folder of photos of him on her computer? How the hell was he supposed to do that? Especially because, as she'd just admitted, she couldn't even remember taking them.

He didn't know much about photography, but even he could see the pictures Riley had taken on Craig and Annie's wedding day were on a whole different level than your ordinary wedding photos. She'd captured special moments, frozen endearing gestures; every single one was a testimony to his sister and her husband's love for each other.

And then there were the photos she'd taken of him. There hadn't been time to study them, but from what he'd seen at a glance, she'd caught every emotion he'd experienced throughout the day, whether he was happy or deep in thought or looking at his sister—it was scary to know Riley had seen right through all his defenses to his vulnerable self.

"Mitch?" Vivian asked as she entered the kitchen. "You okay? You're frowning again. Oh, I know—Uncle Mitch is adding baby to his list of people he worries about." She chuckled as she walked closer.

Putting his arm around his sister, he gave her a hug. "I'm

so happy for you and Aiden. When is baby due?"

"July next year. I'm just about four weeks now. It's early and we probably shouldn't have said anything yet, but we're just so excited and wanted to share the wonderful news with all of you."

"So, we don't know yet whether it's a baby girl or a boy?"

Vivian laughed. "Not before fourteen weeks. We honestly don't mind either way."

"I'd like a baby brother," Dylan said. The little boy had wandered back into the kitchen without being noticed. He was looking up at Mitch and Vivian, the subject of babies clearly one he found fascinating.

"You don't want a sister?" Vivian asked as she crouched down to speak to Dylan.

"I like girls, but I'd like a brother to play with." Sighing, he looked at Mitch. "Mitch kissed Mommy, but she doesn't want a husband."

With raised eyebrows, Vivian looked up at Mitch. "Well, you never know, Mommy may just change her mind."

Dylan's face lit up. "A Christmas miracle?"

Chuckling, Vivian got up again. "Exactly."

Quite happy with her answer, Dylan ran away.

"So, Uncle Mitch, we haven't had a chance to talk about you kissing Riley. I didn't even know you liked each other— what happened?"

Annie entered the kitchen. "Oh, there you are... What are you two talking about? Mitch kissing Riley?" she whispered and hurried closer.

"I just asked him about it," Vivian said.

"Mitch?"

"Okay, yes, we've kissed, but as Dylan has just explained, the last thing Riley wants is a husband."

Annie's eyes widened. "Wow, that was a quick jump from kissing to husband? I didn't even know you liked each other."

Vivian nodded. "That's what I said."

Rubbing his face, Mitch sighed. From previous experience, he knew once his sisters started with an inquisition, he didn't stand a chance.

He had to cut this short. "Worrying about the two of you is keeping me busy enough, thank you very much. I don't want to be responsible for someone else."

"You do know we're quite capable of looking after ourselves?" Vivian asked.

"I know, but I'll probably always blame myself for not noticing when you had problems at work or that I didn't know how to help you, Annie, when that freaking Ted Harris dumped you weeks before your wedding."

Annie gave him a hug. "Seriously, Mitch. What has happened to us is called life—these things happen, they make you grow. Besides, if it hadn't been for either of our misfortunes, we wouldn't be here, and we wouldn't have met the men we are married to now. You wouldn't have finished your novel, which by the way, I'll start reading tonight. You are a wonderful brother, but you have my permission to stop worrying about me."

"About me, too." Vivian grinned. "So, do you have a thing for Riley?"

Annie leaned forward. "Yeah, Mitch, do you?"

Mitch opened and closed his mouth a few times, not sure what to say. Fortunately, his two brothers-in-law entered the kitchen at that moment looking for their wives. He was off the hook. For the moment at least.

Maybe Riley was right—he should just forget what he'd seen on her computer. She was very adamant about not being interested in a relationship.

So, all he had to do was forget how soft her mouth was, how perfectly she fitted against his body, and how alive she made him feel, and all would be well.

Question was—how was he supposed to do that when she was stuck in his mind and on his heart?

He stilled. Heart? Where the hell did that come from?

Cussing softly, he joined the rest of the party around the dining room table. Riley was standing at the other side of the table and was talking to her cousin, studiously ignoring him.

His eyes fell on the telltale blush creeping up her neck, and he grinned. He wasn't the only one who was going to have a bad night, it seemed.

Chapter Ten

BY THE TIME they arrived at Vivian and Aiden's house for lunch on Sunday, Riley was a wreck. She'd thought Mitch would want to talk to her or call her or at least text her, but since they'd left Annie's yesterday, she hadn't heard a word from him.

They were late, and both Mitch's and Aiden's cars were already parked in front of the beautifully renovated house Vivian had fallen in love with earlier this year.

"Everyone is already here." Aunt Janice smiled. "I thought you'd never come out of your room this morning."

"I'm sorry," Riley mumbled as they got out of the car. "I… um… I couldn't decide what to wear. It's never this cold in Portland."

"You look gorgeous." Aunt Janice's eyes twinkled. She obviously knew the reason why Riley had struggled to find something to wear had absolutely nothing to do with the weather and everything to do with Mitch.

Riley sighed. This whole thing with Mitch was driving her crazy. She loved clothes and had figured out long ago she felt most comfortable in informal but feminine items, a kind of boho vibe. She didn't buy many clothes, and usually she felt good in anything in her closet, but today, she couldn't decide what to wear. Every time she'd put something on, she'd looked at herself through Mitch's eyes. Seriously. Eventually she'd settled for a blue polka-dot crossover top with jeans and boots and a pair of dangling blue earrings.

"Wow, it's freezing," Riley gasped. "How do you get used to this?"

Aunt Janice took Dylan's hand as they walked to the front door. "It's cold, I agree, but I've learned to love winter. Everything slows down, you know? You get a chance to take a breath, enjoy the comforts of your home, and just move at a slower pace. And there is always the possibility of a white Christmas. If you come this year, we may just have snow on Christmas Day."

Riley laughed. "Another Christmas miracle?"

Aunt Janice knocked on the door. "Exactly. Miracles do happen, you know."

The door flew opened, and a smiling Aiden wearing an apron motioned them in.

"Are you cooking?" Riley asked.

"He has to." Shaking her head, Vivian approached them. "His wife is a bit useless in the kitchen."

"She makes up for it in many other ways, though," Aiden said, hugging his wife before he removed Dylan's jacket and picked him up.

"Where's the baby?" Dylan asked.

"The baby? Oh…" Aiden smiled. "Aunt Vivian is still carrying it close to her heart. We'll only see it in nine months'… well, probably eight months' time."

Dylan looked at Vivian, clearly puzzled.

Vivian patted her tummy. "The baby still has to grow, sweetie. At this point, it's no bigger than a poppy seed, but in a few months' time, I'll have a round tummy." She motioned with her hands.

"Oh, okay." Dylan nodded as if it all made sense to him. "I'm hungry, Uncle Aiden."

Chuckling, Aiden turned away with Dylan still in his arms. "You know what? So am I. Let's go and see what we can find to eat."

"He's a sharp one." Vivian smiled.

"Has he asked about his own dad yet?" Aunt Janice asked as they left their jackets in the closet next to the front door.

"Not yet, but with all the talk about babies and husbands, he's bound to ask one of these days," Riley said.

They left the hallway and entered the big open-plan kitchen-living room area.

Riley sighed. "Oh, Vivian, I love your house! I still remember the very dilapidated place you bought. You've turned it into a beautiful home like I knew you would. This is so nice." She touched a nativity scene on one of the tables. "Another Christmas fanatic, I see." She chuckled.

"I'm not as bad as Annie, but I do love Christmas." Vivian smiled.

Riley pointed toward a door leading from the living room area. "Are you still involved at the hospital or do you mostly see patients from your offices here?"

"I'm still working part-time at the ER," Vivian said, but as Riley turned around, Mitch was standing right in front her. Everything else, including Vivian's words, faded.

"Hi, Riley." Mitch smiled.

Her mouth was so dry she was worried she wouldn't get a word out. "Hi." It was barely a whisper, but that was all she could manage.

"You haven't seen Mitch's house, have you?" Vivian's voice finally penetrated her foggy brain. "Oh, Mitch, you have to show Riley. He was lucky enough to find a place that has already been renovated. Or haven't you unpacked yet?"

"Of course not," Annie said as she rushed closer. "He had a story to write. Hello, everyone. Oh, I love that we're all together; this is so nice."

"I started reading your story last night," Vivian said to Mitch.

"And?" Mitch asked.

"Interesting plot, believable characters. I particularly liked the character of Dorothy. The way you describe her, I feel I should know her…" Her eyes twinkled.

"I've also read the first couple of chapters," Annie added. "And yes, Dorothy is certainly an interesting character."

"Well, I'm waiting for your feedback while I'm editing," Mitch said, ignoring their remarks. He turned to Riley. "I can show you my house after lunch if you like. I haven't quite finished unpacking, though, so it's still a bit of a mess."

Riley swallowed. Alone with Mitch in his house… so not a good idea. "Don't worry, it's okay, I don't want to be a bother…"

"Oh, but I insist," Mitch said, touching her arm.

Annie's eyes were dancing with mirth as she leaned against Vivian. "He insists, Viv, did you hear?"

Grateful for Dylan who was tugging on her pants, Riley leaned forward so that her hair could hide the blush rising up her neck. Her heart was galloping away at an alarming rate, and Mitch hadn't even touched her.

BY THE TIME they'd finished lunch, Dylan was playing with toys Vivian kept for her patients in the corner of the big living room.

Aunt Janice got up. "Mitch, why don't you take Riley to look at your house? I'll keep Dylan company and if he gets bored, we'll go for a walk."

"I'll join you," Aiden said and got up. "I can do with stretching my legs after this huge lunch."

Annie pulled on Aiden's sleeve. "Sorry, baby, you're on dishwashing duty."

"But I—"

Pulling him down, Annie kissed him. "I'll miss you."

Craig jumped up. "Then I'll join them."

Laughing, Vivian grabbed Craig's hand. "Sorry, no—I promised Annie we'll help in the kitchen."

"But..."

"Come on."

Both his sisters literally dragged their husbands in the direction of the kitchen.

Aunt Janice chuckled. "If I were you, I'd quickly escape. Don't worry about Dylan, Riley, I love spending time with him."

"It's really not necessary..." Riley began.

"Go on," Aunt Janice said. "The house is close by. You'll be back in no time."

Clearly reluctant, Riley got up. "Okay, but I can't stay long," she said. "I'd rather not leave Dylan, he's my responsibility."

"Of course," Mitch agreed, taking her arm as they walked to the front door.

In silence, he helped her with her jacket before he put on his own.

As they stepped outside, Riley inhaled sharply and huddled in her coat. "I don't know if I could ever get used to the cold."

Taking her hand in his, he led her down the pathway to the street. "You get used to it. It also helps to have the right clothes. One of the first things we did when we arrived in Marietta was to shop for warm clothes. The walk would also warm you up in no time," he said, lacing their fingers. "And I have hot chocolate at home."

"I don't think I could eat or drink anything for a week," Riley said, patting her tummy. "You have two very special sisters."

"Interfering, but yes, I have to agree with you—they're special. And here we are," he said motioning toward the next house.

"That is close by," Riley said as they walked up to the double story.

"I'll probably always feel responsible for my two sisters. I wasn't there for them when they've needed me before. I'm going to make sure that never happens again."

"They are all grown up, you know." Riley chuckled.

"I know. They'll always be my sisters, though."

Riley looked up at the house. "I can see why you bought it. It's been beautifully renovated."

"I think so, too. I just need to finish unpacking." He moved to unlock the door.

"Mitch…"

He stopped and turned to look at her. "Yes?"

"I… I'd like to see your house, but… but I don't want to talk about the photos I took of you."

Eyes twinkling, he unlocked the door and waited for her to enter before he closed it. "Okay."

Riley moved farther into the house, and he followed her. "This is the kitchen, dining, and living room."

Riley turned around. "It's really nice, Mitch. What is upstairs?"

He took her hand again. "The bedrooms. I have moved into one. The other two are still without any furniture. Riley?"

She glanced quickly at him.

"We are going to have that conversation about the pictures you took of me at some point, whether you want to or not."

Shaking her head, she tried to pull her hand out of his, but he wasn't ready to lose the contact.

"We don't have to talk about it right now, but I think it warrants a discussion."

Ignoring him, she turned toward the stairs. "Show me what's upstairs?"

They walked up the stairs in silence. The only indication Riley wasn't as cool and collected as she'd like him to believe was the slight trembling of her hand in his.

As they reached the top, Riley quickly pulled her hand out of his and walked toward the two smaller bedrooms to the left. "So which one is your bedroom?"

"This side." He motioned as he turned to walk toward his bedroom.

"Mitch, I…"

He stopped and turned.

"I… can't."

"Can't what?" he asked, walking back to where she was

standing.

"Can't go into your bedroom."

He touched her hand. "Why not?"

She exhaled. "You know why."

He cupped her cheek. "You scared I'll kiss you?"

"Yes... no..." Inhaling deeply, she closed her eyes for a moment before she looked at him again. "We won't stop with just a kiss, and if we're in your room, near your bed..."

He lowered his head. "So, if I kiss you here, far away from my bedroom..." His lips found hers. It was supposed to be a quick kiss, just to tease her, but she angled her head, her mouth opened, and he was lost.

WITH A SIGH, Riley's hand sneaked around Mitch's neck. What the man could do to her with just a kiss...

With a groan, he pulled her even closer, making her aware of his need for her. Big hands stroked her sides, igniting little fires in their wake. When she was just about ready to burst into flames, he cupped her breasts, teasing her nipples with his thumbs.

He lifted his head, his eyes feverish. "I have to touch you..." With those strange eyes never leaving her face, he traced the line of her breasts above the V-neckline of the crossover top.

Her breath hitched; her body shuddered. With a small

smile, he slipped a hand into her top. Flesh on flesh, heat on heat.

Desire raced through her blood, crawled up her throat, and nearly frantic, she pulled down his head again. This time, their lips met in a desperate dance. But it wasn't enough, not nearly enough. She had to get closer to him, touch him, become a part of him.

Tugging at his shirt, her hands found warm skin, toned muscles. Her heart sighed. This was what she'd wanted since forever.

The next moment, Mitch lifted his head, his breathing ragged. "Your phone…"

It took her another minute to hear her phone ringing over the roaring in her ears. Gulping in deep breaths, she tried to find her phone in the pocket of her jeans, but her hands were so unsteady, she couldn't get to it.

Pushing her hands aside, Mitch took out her phone, his hand scraping against her over-sensitive breasts again.

With her eyes locked with his, she answered the phone. "It's Riley…"

"Sweetie, I think you need to come back." It was Aunt Janice's voice.

A cold fist clutched around Riley's throat, nearly cutting off her breath. "Dylan? Is he…?" Her breath got stuck somewhere in her throat, and she couldn't utter another word.

"What's the matter?" Mitch asked.

"I… I… On my way," she got out.

Turning around, she stormed down the stairs. She had to get to Dylan. Right this minute.

Mitch reached the door before her. "Riley, what's wrong?"

"Dylan," she said, the first tear rolling down her cheek.

Mitch grabbed their jackets, gave Riley hers, and while pulling on his own, he opened the door, pushed her out, and locked it behind him. Taking her hand, he jogged down the steps. "Is he—"

"I don't know."

Without talking, they ran down the street toward Vivian and Aiden's house.

She should've been with Dylan, not kissing and making out with Mitch Miller. She had a child; she wasn't a hormone-filled teenager any longer.

Halfway back, she realized she was still clutching his hand and quickly dropped it. As she slowed down when they reached the house, Mitch took her arm.

"Let me…"

"Don't…"

"You want everyone to see what we've been doing?" He reached out to pull her top into place.

Face flaming, Riley turned away and opened the door.

"That's not… your hair."

Combing her fingers through her hair, she opened the door. "Aunt Janice? Vivian? Where—"

"In here, sweetie," Aunt Janice called.

Riley ran toward her voice. Dylan was sitting on Aunt Janice's lap, Vivian was sitting next them, her statoscope on his chest.

Inhaling deeply, Riley tried to keep calm. She should've been here. What kind of mother left her child to go kissing someone she had no business kissing?

"What's wrong?" Riley asked as she reached them.

"I'm not sure. He has a fever," Vivian said. "It could be nothing, but I'm not taking any chances. I'm taking him to the hospital for tests."

"What tests?" Riley asked, her breath coming out in gasps.

Vivian got up and hugged her. "I'm sure it's nothing, but I want to take a urine sample to rule out a UTI…"

"What's that?"

"Urinary tract infection. Maybe also do a CXR… an X-ray of the chest to make sure it's not pneumonia. And… well, we'll see. Kids sometimes develop a high fever for seemingly no reason—we talk about pyrexia of unknown origin. I promise we'll do everything we can."

"I'll take him," Mitch said, and before Riley could protest, he had Dylan in his arms. "Craig? You driving?"

"We'll follow you," Aiden said as he took a very pale Aunt Janice by the hand.

Chapter Eleven

EARLY MONDAY MORNING, Dylan's fever finally broke. Light-headed from relief, Riley sagged down on the chair next to his bed in the ER.

Vivian put a hand on Riley's shoulder. "We'll get the results from the blood tests today, but I'm fairly certain it's nothing major, so you can take Dylan home. I've texted Aunt Janice already—she's expecting you. I'm sure there's a huge breakfast waiting on the two"—she glanced at Mitch—"or three of you."

Dylan sat upright. "I'm hungry, Mommy."

Swallowing back her tears, Riley grabbed his hand. "I'm so happy to hear that."

Mitch stepped forward. "I'll drive you and Dylan back."

Dylan reached out to Mitch, obviously comfortable to let Mitch pick him up.

"Come on, big guy, I'm so happy to see that smile."

With a sigh, Dylan put his head against Mitch's broad chest, obviously feeling safe in the big man's arms.

Overwhelmed, alarmed, and also scared by the scene of her small son in Mitch's gentle hug, Riley jumped up. "I can take Dylan; we'll be okay. It's Monday morning. You have to go to work soon. I'll get Aiden to come and pick me up."

Ignoring her, he walked to the door.

"Let him do this," Vivian said softly. "He hasn't left your side throughout the night, never mind how many times I've told him there wasn't anything he could do. He's a caretaker, so let him take care of you and Dylan?"

Dazed, Riley stared at Vivian. She'd been so focused on Dylan she'd barely registered anything else around her. Aunt Janice had left with Aiden and Annie at some point, and she'd thought Mitch had left with them.

Nodding, Riley hugged Vivian. "Thank you so much for all you've done. I hope you can get some sleep before you see patients."

Vivian grinned. "I don't work on Mondays, except if there's a crisis. You must be exhausted; I hope both you and Dylan can get some sleep. I'll let you know as soon as I hear from the pathologists. Go, go, Mitch is probably already in the car."

RILEY WAS QUIET all the way back to Janice's house. She'd insisted on sitting in the back with Dylan and was cradling the little boy close to her. In the rearview mirror, she looked pale and worried.

Trying to concentrate on his driving, Mitch focused on

the street in front of him. It wasn't quite seven o'clock and still quiet. In a small town like Marietta, there were no traffic jams to take into account when you drove anywhere, exactly what he'd had in mind when he'd discussed the idea to move away from Sacramento with his sisters.

He was living exactly the kind of life he'd dreamed about. There were no deadlines, no chasing after the next big client, no office parties he needed to attend. Teaching math hadn't been something he'd even considered when he'd left school, but his mom had insisted he get a teacher's qualification, as well. He often wished he could thank her for her insight. She'd known him better than he'd known his twenty-year-old self.

He'd been strangely restless over the last few months. He couldn't put his finger on why he felt that way. He'd finally sat down and written his novel. Hopefully, he'd be able to send it to a publisher soon. Teaching came naturally to him, and he enjoyed the kids, enjoyed listening to their ideas, discussing it with them. His sisters were both happy and thriving; he should've been content, but he hadn't been.

Not until… Turning his head, he looked at Riley. Not until he'd seen her again. Since her arrival, he was strangely excited as if he was waiting for something extraordinary to happen.

As he parked on the driveway of Janice's house, the front door flew open. Janice was already dressed for work. She rushed closer as Mitch got out of the car. "Oh, I'm so happy

Dylan is better. Come on in, I've made breakfast. Mitch? I hope you can stay?"

Riley opened her door and, ignoring his hand to help, also got out of the car. "I'm sure Mitch wants to get home, Aunt Janice. He has to get ready for work."

Dylan scrambled out after her. "I'm better, Aunt Janice!" he called out as he ran toward her.

"Oh, I'm so happy. Come on, I've made pancakes." The two of them disappeared into the house.

Riley turned to him. "Thanks, Mitch."

He took her hand, and she stepped back quickly.

"I… I can't do this, Mitch. I shouldn't have left Dylan last night. Look what happened to him while I was making out like a schoolgirl."

Chuckling, Mitch reached out and touched her face. "A very sexy schoolgirl, may I add? Dylan didn't develop a fever because you weren't there. And you left him with people who care about him."

Her eyes cast downward, Riley clutched her handbag against her body. "He's my responsibility; I'm his mom. I should've been there for him. Good-bye, Mitch. I don't think it's a good idea for me to see you again before we go back."

"So, you want me to forget there is a folder full of photographs of me on your laptop? Forget I had my hands all over you last night?"

Her eyes flew to his, and just for a moment, he saw the

flash of desire he'd witnessed in his house the night before.

She quickly looked away again, though, fidgeting with her bag. "This thing—whatever it is—between us has no future, you know that. We live in two different states, we have different responsibilities; the whole idea is ridiculous. And anyway, I won't be able to trust anyone again, let alone have a relationship with—"

Before she could finish her sentence, he'd bent down and kissed her. Her mouth was cold, unmoving, but angling his head, he deepened the kiss. Within seconds, she was clinging to him, her mouth soft, yielding.

Only then he lifted his head. "You're not getting rid of me that easily. Go and sleep. I'll see you later."

Her eyes were still dazed when he got into his car. With a last wave, he drove away.

She was right, he knew it. A relationship between the two of them was ludicrous, but what he felt when he was near her was real, damn it. How was he supposed to forget about it?

What exactly it was, he was still trying to figure out, but he wasn't ready to walk away just yet. He'd give her some space—he had a busy week ahead anyway—but at some point, they'd need to have a conversation about all those photos of him on her laptop. And there was the very obvious attraction between the two of them, not something that could be ignored.

He could see in her eyes she wanted him the same way he

wanted her. Question was, what should he do about it? More importantly, did he want to do something about it when she so clearly wasn't interested in taking this any further?

ON WEDNESDAY AFTERNOON Riley took a deep breath as she parked her car in front of Annie and Craig's house. Since Dylan's trip to the ER on Sunday, she hadn't slept properly. She was tired, fretful, close to tears the whole time, and so irritated with herself because she was feeling like this. What was wrong with her?

Dylan was fine, Vivian had said, so she could relax. Not even the good news about her son had been able to restore her spirits, though.

Worried Dylan wouldn't want to stay at school, she'd accompanied Janice yesterday when they'd taken Dylan to join the prekindergarten class. When she'd picked him up later in the day, he had a new friend. This morning the mother was waiting for them and Dylan was invited to his first playdate in Marietta. It was easy to agree, Janice knew the family.

Annie's invitation to come for tea couldn't have come at a better time. She actually had time for grown-up conversation and she didn't have to worry about Dylan.

While Dylan had been at school, she'd also finally had time to finish Annie and Aiden's wedding photos yesterday.

This was a great opportunity to let Annie pick the ones she'd like to have in print, as well.

Besides worrying about her son since Sunday, her mind had also been filled with Mitch. Apart from a text to ask how Dylan was, she hadn't heard from him since he'd left her Monday morning. She should be relieved—it was what she'd wanted, what she'd asked for. So why was she still dreaming about his kisses, his warm hands, his soft smile, the tender way he was with her son?

Aaargh, this is not helping.

As she jumped out of her car, the front door opened.

Annie waved at her. "Hello, it's so nice to see you! Where's Dylan?"

"At his first playdate."

"Really?"

"Yes. Dylan has made a friend on his very first day and has a playdate. Mike… somebody."

"That's wonderful," Annie said. "He didn't sound too happy about school when I asked him." Annie took Riley's coat as she ushered her inside.

"You're right," Riley said. "But apparently this school is way nicer. The teacher smiles, he tells me."

"Great news. And Vivian tells me he's okay. Apparently, his blood tests were all fine?"

"Yes, I can't tell you how relieved I was to hear that," Riley said as they entered Annie big kitchen. "It has been such a scary experience. I've also been online, and as Vivian says, kids sometimes get these unexplained fevers. It's wonderful to have a sister-in-law who is a doctor."

"I know, right? Come and sit. I've made scones with the tea. Thanks again for the gorgeous photos. Craig and I relived every moment of our wedding day last night while looking through them. You have such a wonderful talent, Riley—we're so blessed that you've agreed to take our wedding pictures."

"Of course, we're family. I can't ever repay Craig for what he's done for me. This is my small way of thanking him and thanking you for making him so happy."

Sniffling, Annie motioned to a chair. "Now you've made me cry. Sit down, let's have tea."

Riley touched Annie's hand before she sat down. "Thanks for inviting me. As you've probably gathered by now, I'm not big on crowds and seldom go anywhere. My best friend back in Portland, the one who kept me from becoming a complete recluse, is now married, so I rarely go out to have a cup of tea and a chat with a friend in the middle of the week. I should probably make new friends."

"Or you could move to Marietta." Annie smiled.

Riley shook her head. "Our home, our life is back in Portland. Please remember my offer to have copies printed of whatever photos you like." Riley was deliberately changing the subject, but moving to Marietta was not something she wanted to talk about.

Annie didn't say anything, just smiled. "Thanks, I'll

think about it, but as you know, Bozeman is quite close by. I've discovered a place in the city that could do it for us."

"Okay, great, but do let me know if I can help."

While drinking tea, they talked about general things for a few minutes until Annie put her cup down.

"You can tell me to mind my own business, but I have to ask—is there something going on between you and my brother?"

Riley sighed. "You're not about to mind your own business, never mind what I say, are you?"

"Nope." Annie grinned.

"Even if there is something—and I'm not saying there is—it probably has more to do with the fact that I haven't been with somebody since I discovered I was pregnant four years ago. You have to be dead not to see Mitch is"—blushing, she inhaled deeply—"attractive, and I'm not dead. I can't just blindly fall for someone living miles away, though. I have Dylan to think about. Besides, I don't see myself trusting anyone ever again. Relationships, marriage—I've had my chance."

"Oh, nonsense," Annie called out. "You're what… thirty?"

"Thirty-two," Riley said.

"You're barely out of your twenties. You can't stop living and loving because one idiot let you down. Did you actually love him?"

Riley grimaced. "I thought so at the time, but looking

back, I think we just sort of drifted toward the idea of getting married. There was no great passion, not like there is…"

"Between you and Mitch?"

"I was going to say, not like there is between you and Craig, and Vivian and Aiden. What you guys have is so rare; it's not something you see every day. Percy realized we didn't have it before I did. Although, it would've been nice if he hadn't waited for our wedding day to tell me or at least had the decency to talk to me in person."

Annie nodded. "You remember I was dumped weeks before my wedding day, as well. For a long time, I didn't think I deserved to be happy, that I'd never marry, but Riley, life happens. You can't deny yourself happiness because you're afraid you'll be hurt again."

"You're right. And when I'm back in Portland, I'll consider dating again."

Annie leaned forward and touched Riley's arm. "Are you telling me you're going to ignore the obvious spark between you and Mitch and date someone else?"

"I live in a different state, Annie. As you know, when our parents died, Aunt Janice was wonderful. She moved in with us and tried her best to make a home for us, but for me, the house was never the same. And then when I was dumped and found out I was pregnant, my life kinda fell apart. I had no control over anything—I don't ever want to feel like that again. After Dylan was born, I used my inheritance to buy a house. I wanted to have… needed to have a place I could call home again. I'm finally at the point where I have that, where I have order in my life, where I know exactly what is happening when. We have a life in Portland. I can't just up and go because a seriously sexy guy kissed me."

"Seriously sexy, huh?" Annie laughed.

Blushing, Riley groaned. "You know what I mean."

"I do." Annie nodded. "Craig and Aiden had the same problem, but both of them found an easy solution. They moved to Marietta, leaving everything behind to be with the women they love."

Riley's hand shook, and she quickly put her cup down. "See? They've fallen in love. Entirely different situations."

"Is it, though?" Annie chuckled. "But only you know what's in your heart. Life, I've discovered, can't always be controlled. Unforeseen things happen—Aunt Janice may get ill, as you've thought. Dylan suddenly developed a fever. Difference is, when you're living here, we're all there to help."

Riley was shaking her head even before Annie had finished speaking. "I can't… I just can't." Time to talk about something else. "So, tell me about your guesthouse? Are you still happy with the number of guests you're getting? Remember, I'm here until Friday. I can easily take more photographs if you like?"

Annie laughed. "Changing the subject, are we? It won't always work, you know. I'm here if you ever want to talk. Okay, different topic. Yes, the guesthouse has been gloriously busy over the summer, I'm happy to report. On occasion, I've actually had to tell people I don't have a room for them. Do you really think it's necessary to change the pictures on my website? Craig has mentioned the idea, too, but I don't know whether there's a point."

Riley nodded. "Maybe bring a little winter and Christmas to your pages? You've turned your house into a Christmas wonderland—I think you should show people what it looks like this time of year. And what about pictures of Main Street at night? Copper Mountain covered in snow? And isn't there a lake somewhere where you skate? I remember Aiden mentioning it."

Annie clapped her hands. "Miracle Lake. Oooh, yes, it sounds lovely. Maybe we can all go one evening. It's freezing cold, but they serve hot chocolate, and we don't have to stay long. Dylan would love it. But do you have time?"

"It'll have to be tomorrow—we're leaving on Friday, but I should be able to do quite a lot during a day. I can take the other pictures in the morning, and then maybe if we go to Miracle Lake tomorrow, after everyone is back from work, I could take a few pictures there?"

Annie grabbed her phone. "Sounds perfect. Let me text everyone. I'll make something so we can have a light supper before we go."

Chapter Twelve

MITCH WAS ON his way back from school when he saw Riley's car in front of Annie's house. He was going to swing by Janice's house later to talk to her, but he wasn't going to waste another moment before he could see her.

The last two days had been busy at school. Also, both his sisters had finished reading his manuscript, and each one had sent him notes and ideas as he'd requested. He wasn't sleeping anyway, so the last two nights he hadn't even tried. Instead of rolling around in bed, dreaming about a long-legged redhead who was driving him nuts, he'd been editing his manuscript.

With a quick knock on the front door, he opened it. "Annie?" he called.

His sister appeared in the kitchen door. "Come on in, I've made scones."

Smiling, he gave his sister a quick hug. "Thanks, sounds nice. Thanks for all your notes, by the way. I appreciate your help."

"I loved the story," she said as they entered the kitchen. "Not difficult to guess who your inspiration for Dorothy is," she said under her breath. "Riley and I are having tea."

His eyes found Riley's, and his heart sighed. Damn, he'd missed seeing her face. Without conscious thought, he walked up to where she was sitting and touched her shoulder. "Hey, you. I was going to stop by Janice's later, but then I saw your car outside…" Bending down, he kissed her.

The sound of her breath hitching in her throat nearly brought him to his knees, and he simply had to feel the satiny texture of her face beneath his fingers. Her eyes darkened.

He had to clear his throat before he could speak. "Is Dylan with Janice?"

"He's… um… he's at a playdate." Her voice was husky and not quite steady.

Mmm, she was also a bit rattled, he was happy to see. "So, he likes school?"

"This one, apparently," Annie said. "Maybe a good idea to leave him with Janice as she suggested when you go back for your photo shoot."

"I don't think I'm coming back for Christmas, Annie. I have a lot of work…"

"You should make sure you're back a few days before the big day," Annie said, blithely ignoring Riley. "There are so many things happening close to Christmas Dylan would enjoy. There's a gingerbread house competition; we're all putting up Christmas trees and would need help, not to mention all the cooking to be done before the big day.

Christmas is a time for family, and you're family, Riley. Your and Dylan's place is here, with us. Tea, Mitch?"

Nodding, Mitch sat down next to Riley. "You might as well agree." He grinned at Riley. "Annie will not stop pestering you, if you don't."

Annie had already moved on to the next topic. "Riley sent us the final wedding photos last night—I'm so happy with every single one. You've captured exceptional moments in such a special way, Riley. Mitch, there's such a beautiful one of you and Dylan at the reception…"

"They're all extraordinary." He looked at Riley. "I've wanted to ask you—the photo of Dylan and me in front of the cottonwood tree, will you please send it to me?" Mitch looked down at his tea. "It's probably saved in the other folder on your computer."

The only indication Riley had heard him was a quick intake of breath. "I'll have a look." As she put her cup down, she got up. "I really have to go, Annie. I still have to pick up Dylan. Thanks for a lovely afternoon. I'll see what I can do tomorrow about new pictures of the town in all its Christmas glory."

"Thank you. And we'll see all of you at around six? Mitch, did you get my text?"

Mitch took out his phone. "I keep it on silent during school hours."

"Riley is going to take more pictures for my website. We thought of going to Miracle Lake tomorrow after you all have finished work. I do love the vibe of the place."

Riley turned away. "Okay, great, we'll see you there. Dylan has never skated before; he'll be fascinated."

Mitch placed a hand at Riley's back. "I'll walk her out," he told Annie.

"I'm perfectly capable of walking myself to the door." Riley huffed as they reached the front door. Opening the door, she stepped out onto the porch.

"Of course, you are," he said. "But then I wouldn't get the chance to do this…"

He bent down until their lips were nearly touching. "I could really do with another kiss."

Big blue eyes looked up at him. "You drive me crazy!" Grabbing hold of his shirt, she stood on her toes and kissed him. "You can't keep kissing me!"

He took her hand in his. "May I please take you out to dinner Friday night?"

"We're leaving Friday morning."

Frowning, he stared down at her. "Why not stay the weekend?"

"I work on Sunday."

"What about tonight?"

Crossing her arms, she sighed. "I don't think it's a good idea."

"It's dinner, Riley."

"Not tonight. I don't want to leave Dylan alone just yet. After Sunday, I'm still a bit worried about him."

"What about a drink tomorrow night after we've been to Miracle Lake?"

"I have Dylan…"

"I'll wait while you put him to bed. You've run out of excuses, Riley."

Rolling her eyes, she sighed. "Okay, but it'll have to be a quick one. We'll have to be on the road early Friday morning to be on time for our flight."

The tight band around his chest loosened ever so slightly. "Okay, see you tomorrow."

Turning around, she jogged down the steps toward her car. He watched her until the taillights of her car disappeared around the corner.

As he turned back, his sister was leaning against the kitchen door. "You're smitten, aren't you?"

Shrugging he nodded. "I like her, she's… feisty."

Annie grinned. "Feisty, uh? Exactly like your Dorothy. So, what are you going to do about it?"

"There's nothing to do. She's leaving Friday, and I don't think she's planning to be back for Christmas."

"Well, then. You'll just have to change her mind, won't you? Why don't you send her your story? I'm sure she's going to like Dorothy."

"You done interfering in my life?"

"Not by a long shot." Annie laughed.

By eleven o'clock on Thursday morning, Riley had taken hundreds of photos of Main Street. She'd had a lovely morning. All the shops were lit up, Christmas music was blaring from all sides, and everyone she'd met was friendly and warm.

She'd had coffee in Java Café, met interesting characters, and had even been asked to photograph the local firemen for a calendar for charity. At the flower shop, she'd met Risa, the owner, who seemed to know quite a bit about Riley's brother and cousin.

As she exited the bookshop, she noticed the pharmacy on the opposite corner. A faint headache had been irritating her since early morning; she should pop in for some Tylenol before she continued her exploration of the town. She'd left in such a hurry she didn't even grab her small first aid bag she usually traveled with.

Looking up and down the street before she crossed, she couldn't help a smile. Although it was in the middle of the day, and the shops and businesses were all open, there was hardly any traffic and very few people around—the ideal setting for introverts like her.

Since she'd begun her stroll down Main Road, she hadn't experienced the feeling of claustrophobia she often got when shopping in Portland. The town was quiet, peaceful, everyone moving at a much slower pace than what she usually saw in the city. People weren't rushing past each other, not noticing anything else like they did in the city. They stopped and actually talked to one another.

There were a few people in the pharmacy, but she couldn't find anyone to help her. The only woman who seemed to work there was behind the counter, talking on the phone, loud enough for all to hear.

"Really? You don't say?" The woman inhaled sharply, her eyes widening. "I don't believe it…"

After another few *oohs* and *aahs*, Riley leaned forward. "Excuse me…"

The woman had seen her, but it was clear she wasn't about to end the conversation anytime soon.

"Is there someone else who can help me?" Riley asked again.

The woman's eyes narrowed. "Betty, I'll call you back just now; another O'Sullivan just walked in. Hmm, the very same."

"Tylenol, please?" Riley asked.

With a nod, the woman turned around to look for it on one of the shelves behind her.

"How do you know who I am?" Riley asked, trying to be friendly.

With a sniff, the woman put the bottle in a small paper bag. "The red hair. I hear Mitch Miller can't keep his hands to himself around you."

Riley inhaled sharply, aware of the blush creeping up her neck. "I beg your pardon?"

"And Betty has heard he's kissed you right there on his

sister's porch."

Completely thrown, Riley threw bills on the counter before she stormed out of the pharmacy. Outside, she bumped into Risa from the flower shop.

Risa grabbed Riley's arm to steady her. "Don't tell me— you've met the town gossip, Carol Bingley?"

"That's Carol Bingley? Of course, it all makes sense now." Rubbing her face, Riley exhaled. "So it's really true what they say about small towns?"

Risa laughed. "That everyone knows everything about your business?"

Still rattled, Riley nodded. "Yes, that. And I have just been thinking it may not be such a bad idea to live in a small town."

Smiling, Risa touched her hand. "You get used to it. What is also true, though, is that when you're in any kind of trouble, every single person in this town would go out of their way to help you."

"She knows I've kissed Mitch!" Riley cried out. Only after the words had left her mouth, she realized what she'd said.

Risa chuckled. "Everyone in town knows that by now. Who kisses whom around here is high on the list of topics for the gossipers. If you don't want anyone to talk about you, rather do your kissing behind closed doors."

"I'm not kissing... I mean it was a one-time thing, okay, maybe two or three..."

Risa was shaking with laughter. Stepping forward, she gave Riley a quick hug. "You should seriously think about moving to a small town, to this small town. Lots of kissing going around here." She pointed over Riley's shoulder. "I have to go; there's someone at my shop, but stop by again anytime."

As Risa left, Riley noticed the door of Risa's shop was wide open. "You've left your door unlocked?" she asked.

"Of course. It's a small town," Risa called over her shoulder. "Everybody knows everybody."

As Riley stepped into the street, the sun appeared from behind a cloud, shining on the snowcapped top of Copper Mountain. Beautiful. Inhaling the fresh air, she lifted her camera. The mountain was breathtaking; this one should definitely go up on Annie's website.

Her fingers were still shaking, and she took a few shots before she was happy. Who on earth could've seen Mitch kissing her? And why would anyone rush and tell the rest of the town what he or she had seen?

Back in Portland, she'd met one neighbor, an older woman who'd introduced herself. Sally, if she remembered correctly. She didn't know the others, and she doubted if they were interested in anything she did. They waved and nodded to each other, but no one was bothered enough about anyone else to go around spreading gossip.

Sighing, she walked toward her car. If Risa was right and everyone knew, it meant her brother and cousin had also probably heard about the kiss. Seriously.

Chapter Thirteen

"But, Mo-om," Dylan wailed as Riley picked him up. "I don't wanna go home! I want to skate with Mitch again!"

Riley sighed, waving again to Vivian and Aiden as they walked away. They'd just finished skating, and Dylan was not ready to go. Annie and Craig had left a little earlier as Annie was expecting guests. It had been a long day for her little boy. All the excitement and exercise were finally catching up with Dylan.

They'd had a lovely bowl of soup and homemade bread at Annie's before they'd left for the lake. All through dinner, she and Mitch had to endure her brother and cousin's snide remarks about the kiss *everyone* in town was talking about. Fortunately, Annie and Vivian had managed to calm down their husbands and made a joke of the whole incident. She'd seen the light in the women's eyes, though, and knew at some point she was going to be cornered.

She hugged her son close. "I know, sweetie, but they're going to close in a little while anyway. When we visit Aunt Janice in winter, we'll come again, I promise."

Sniffling, Dylan buried his face in her chest.

Mitch approached. "What's wrong, big guy?" he asked Dylan.

"I wanted to skate with you again," Dylan said.

"Come on," Mitch said and took Dylan from Riley. With one movement, he put Dylan on his neck. "Shall we race your mom and Aunt Janice to the car?"

Tears forgotten, Dylan nodded, excitedly. "Yes, let's run!"

"I'll meet you at the car!" Aunt Janice laughed.

"Come on, Mommy," Dylan called.

"I don't think I have enough energy left." Riley grinned.

"Ahh, Mitch is so good with Dylan, isn't he? You'll have to play along, I'm afraid. Dylan won't forgive you otherwise. Take the key; I'll be there in a minute," Aunt Janice said, thrusting the car keys in Riley's hand. "Just no kissing where everyone can see!" She chuckled.

Ignoring her aunt's remark, Riley ran after them, not an easy task in the snow. She was not going to think about the kiss again.

Aunt Janice was right, Mitch was amazing with Dylan. Her son didn't easily warm to strange men, but he and Mitch had clicked right from the start.

They'd reached the car before she caught up with them.

"We won, Mommy, we won!" Dylan cried, throwing his arms around Mitch's neck.

Shaken, she swallowed against the sudden lump in her

throat. She unlocked the car and opened the back door so that Mitch could put Dylan in his chair. The sight of her son feeling so comfortable with Mitch nearly had her in tears.

Taking great care, Mitch fastened the seat belts around Dylan. "I'm going to miss you," he said, before dropping a kiss on Dylan's head.

"I'll miss you, too, Uncle Mitch."

As Mitch closed the door, Aunt Janice reached them. "Oh, my goodness." She gasped. "I'm completely out of breath. Mitch, why don't you come for a cup of hot chocolate or something?"

Riley felt Mitch's eyes on her. She hadn't told Aunt Janice or any of the others that Mitch had asked her out for a drink. She'd hoped Mitch would forget about his invitation, especially after all the remarks about their kiss.

"Mitch has invited me to go for a drink with him, Aunt Janice. I first want to put Dylan in bed, though." She looked at Mitch. "Give me fifteen minutes?"

Aunt Janice shook her head. "But that's just silly, sweetie. You go with Mitch; I'll put Dylan to bed. It's our last night together, and we have a story to finish, don't we, Dylan?"

"Yes!" Dylan called out.

Riley wavered. She'd thought she'd have time to prepare herself before Mitch would pick her up.

Mitch touched her arm. "I'm happy to pick you up later, if that's what you'd prefer."

She didn't want him to drive home only to have to pick her up again. "Okay, I'll go with you. I just want to say good-bye to Dylan."

A few minutes later, Aunt Janice had left and they were trudging through the snow toward Mitch's car. With every step, her heart rate increased so that by the time they'd reached his car, she was just about hyperventilating. Inhaling deeply, she tried to calm herself. She was having a drink with a family friend. That was it.

Opening the door of the car, Mitch helped her inside, his fingers trailing down her arm before he closed it. Her mouth dried up, the zoo animals in her tummy had to be doing cartwheels or something; she was a shuddering mess. Putting a hand to her abdomen, she tried to focus on her breathing.

Oh, my goodness, this had been such a bad idea. As Mitch got in next to her, strange electric vibes filled the small space, making it difficult to concentrate on anything else besides the big man next to her.

Gulping in a deep breath, she looked out of the side window, but his scent had seeped into her pores, making her light-headed, and she couldn't focus on anything else. The hot, male body next to hers had all her attention.

Fumbling, she took off the warm hat she'd worn. Her hair tumbled down over her shoulders. "I must look a fright." She tried combing her hair with her fingers, but her fingers were shaking so much, she gave up quickly.

Mitch took her hand. "You look beautiful—you always

do. I'm glad you and Annie decided on the idea of skating. It was nice."

She looked down at the white, frilly blouse with tiny buttons down the front she was wearing underneath her coat. When she'd packed, she'd thought she'd be nursing her aunt back to health, not go on dates. This one was one of her favorites, though, and she felt good in it. With it, she was wearing a pair of colorful hoop earrings she hoped would make her look less pale.

"Dylan so enjoyed it," Riley said, trying not to look at Mitch but to keep her gaze on the road in front of them. She'd been just about drooling since she'd seen him at Annie's earlier.

The moment her eyes had met his, her legs turned to rubber. Just looking at him. Dressed in a blue shirt with a pair of tight-fitting denims, he was heart-stoppingly gorgeous. Seriously, she was thirty-two, not thirteen.

"So, how did Dylan's playdate go yesterday?" Mitch asked as they drove away. "In all the excitement of the skating, I never asked him."

"Great. Dylan couldn't stop talking about Mike. Mike this and Mike that—the two had a great time." Riley smiled. "So, where are we having a drink?" She'd been going for cheerful, but the sound coming out of her mouth was more strangled than happy.

"At my place."

The words fell into the air around them. They'd be all

alone; there wouldn't be any other family member around. Just the two of them.

She needed to lighten the mood, joke, anything to keep her from doing something stupid. "You actually have glasses and everything?"

He smiled. "I do. I'll have to get more, but there are at least two chip-free ones we can use."

Minutes later, they arrived at his house. As Mitch got out of the car, she took another deep breath. *Help!*

Mitch took her hand, sending a delicious shiver down her spine.

"Are you cold?" he asked as they reached the front door. "It's nice and warm inside, I promise."

She couldn't tell him she wasn't shivering from cold but from wanting him so badly she could barely see straight.

Inside, it was indeed nice and warm, and she took off her jacket. Mitch had gotten rid of his and reached out to take hers. Their fingers met, and they both froze. Those extraordinary eyes darkened, and the air around them thickened, making breathing difficult.

Without looking at what he was doing, he dropped her jacket, stepped closer. "I want to be with you Riley; I ache for you. It's not why I've brought you here, though, so if…"

Far away, a little voice was trying to warn her, but ignoring it, her hands slipped around his head. "Kiss me, please?" She wanted this, wanted Mitch with an overwhelming desire.

He cupped her face. "With pleasure, ma'am." For another torturing second, his eyes roamed feverishly over her face before, with a guttural growl, his lips met hers.

With a sigh, she sank into the kiss, reveling in the urgency of his mouth, his rock-hard muscles under her fingers. Within minutes, though, heat slammed into her, sending her blood racing through her body. His intoxicating scent, the urgency of his hands, the sound of his ragged breathing were all sending her senses into overdrive.

His lips slid over her face, kissing, tasting every inch while those clever hands ran over her, torturing her, leaving her aching for him. She was burning up, her heart hammering like a runaway train. It was too much, not nearly enough.

Whimpering, she opened enough buttons on his shirt to be able to touch him. The need to get her hands on him was so overwhelming she'd finally stopped listening to the screaming little voice in her head.

LIFTING HIS HEAD, Mitch gulped in some much-needed oxygen. His hands were unsteady, his body on fire; he'd never wanted anyone this desperately.

"I... bed..." he stammered as she undid another button and pressed her lips against him.

"Too far..." she said in between kisses, her arms sliding around him.

Barking out a laugh, he tugged his shirt over his head.

Sighing, she spread her hands over his abdomen. "Wow, a real six-pack…" she breathed.

"I need to see you, too," he got out, his hands anxiously pulling her top from her jeans. He reached out to undo the first button, but his fingers were so unsteady, he struggled to complete the simple task.

"Let me…" Her breath ragged, her gorgeous blue eyes darkened by desire, she stepped back and got rid of her top, as well.

Light-headed, his eyes raked over her, trying to take in every detail. Pale pink satin and lace cupped generous breasts. "Beautiful," he breathed, trailing his fingers down her arms, his eyes feasting on the luminous texture of her skin while he desperately tried to rein in his galloping libido.

With a groan, he captured her lips again. He'd wanted to go slow, to drink in every moment, but Riley's busy hands were driving him beyond the point where he could think. For too long, he'd tried to ignore this ache low in his belly; he was quickly losing control.

He swept an arm under her legs, and swallowing her whimper, he picked her up, staggered toward the living room where he kneeled and put her down on the carpet.

"I… I have to warn you"—she raised herself on her elbows—"I'm not very good at this."

Lying down beside her, he tried to unhook her bra, but he struggled; he was too eager, his hands too slow in obeying messages from his brain. Her breath ragged like his, her hands moved to her back, and in seconds, her gorgeous breasts spilled out. "I don't know what idiot led you to believe that, but you're very good at making me ache for you."

"Ache." She moaned. "I love that."

His hands trembled in anticipation; he was finally able to touch her without any barrier. Moving restlessly below him, Riley whimpered. That was all the encouragement he needed. Bending down, his mouth closed over her breast. Her fingers slid into his hair, keeping him close to her.

With infinite care, he suckled and loved her breasts until her nipples hardened, her heart tripped under his fingers.

Her body arched up, and his hand slid down over petal-soft skin, paying close attention to every soft curve, every toned line. Smooth, hot, tantalizing.

He was never going to get enough of her.

NEARLY FRANTIC, RILEY'S hands moved to his jeans; she wanted to touch him without any barrier between them. The urgency driving her to get even closer to him wouldn't let up. Legs tangled as she tried in vain to get rid of his clothes.

"You're killing me," he got out before he kissed her, his tongue shooting straight through to meet hers in a desperate dance.

For a little while longer, he tortured her before he quickly got rid of his jeans. Lying back next to her, he kept his eyes on her as he unsnapped her jeans. "You sure about this?"

She didn't answer him, couldn't answer him. Desire had dried out her mouth, scrambled her brain; saying anything remotely logical wasn't possible. Lifting her hips, she tried to get out of her own jeans.

"Let me…" He took over from her.

Inch by delicious inch, he peeled down her jeans, pulled off her boots, until all she was left wearing was the small triangle of satin and lace.

"Beautiful." Leaning forward, his hand glided up her legs, paying attention to her calves, her knees before it slowly, so slowly moved closer to where she needed him most.

Her breath caught somewhere in her throat. She felt beautiful, desirable, probably for the first time in her life.

"These"—bending down, his lips followed his hands up her legs—"these gorgeous legs of yours have been driving me crazy for months. Do you have any idea how many nights I've dreamed of being here with you, like this?"

His eyes burned hot. Strange, in this moment, they were the same dark color. That was her last rational thought. With a quick movement, he tugged the last barrier away.

Lifting his eyes, he grinned. "I have to repeat, you're very, very good at this."

In that moment, she felt like the most beautiful woman on planet Earth. She wanted to touch him, but he leaned forward until his mouth found her aching heat.

With his name on her lips, she arched up into his kiss, giving herself to him.

※

WITH HIS BLOOD roaring in his head, Mitch tasted her, caressed her, loved her with his mouth and hands until, with a low moan, her body arched up, and shuddering, she cried out his name. Moving back over her damp skin, he watched in awe as she reached the first peak.

The room was in shadows; the rest of the world had disappeared. Around them, the air had thickened, making breathing difficult. The fire burning low in his belly, urging him to become a part of her, was fast becoming unbearable.

As she opened her eyes again, he hoisted himself above her. He'd never wanted anyone this desperately before.

"I need to be with you. Look at me?" He got out and watched those beautiful eyes open. She lifted her arms.

This moment, this place, being here with Riley—it would forever be a part of him. He'd been waiting for this forever.

With one thrust, he slid into her. Her heat clamped around him like a velvet glove, welcoming him home. Grabbing hold of his shoulders, she sobbed out his name as he began to move. Within seconds, she'd found his rhythm, and with their eyes locked, together they raced up a steep hill.

Bending down, he crushed his mouth down on hers again, swallowed her sigh, and immersed in her softness, he let go of the reins. Soft limbs wrapped around him, and with his face buried in her hair, they finally crested together.

RILEY WAS FAST asleep and breathing deeply. Mitch had been awake for a while, staring at her. They'd finally made it to his room, and he couldn't stop looking at the woman in his bed, her red hair spread out over his pillow as he'd been dreaming about for so long.

Reaching over, he picked up her phone, checked the time before he put it back again. Morning would arrive way too soon, but they still had time.

Her eyes fluttered open. "Mitch?" she breathed.

"I'm here. I'll always be here, waiting for you. I've been waiting for you forever," he whispered before he kissed her again.

Chapter Fourteen

BY THE TIME Dylan was finally dressed on Friday morning, he was in tears and Riley very close to having a meltdown herself. It was hard just putting one foot in front of the other, when every delicious moment of the previous night kept running through her mind, over and over.

Her insides were still shaking. She and Mitch had been together. They'd made love. Not once, not twice but… Inhaling shakily, she tried to remember how many times Mitch had reached for her, but her memory was a haze of tangled limbs and heavy breathing.

And then she'd snuck out of Mitch's house without saying good-bye and ran back to Janice's house in the bitter cold. It was a lousy thing to do, she knew it, but there was no way she could face him and not throw herself in his arms again, begging him to let her stay.

I'm here. I'll always be here, waiting for you. I've been waiting for you forever—the words Mitch had whispered to her last night, refused to go away; they were seared into her memory forever.

He had to go to work, she had to plane to catch, and life

was moving on, despite the earth-shattering experience in Mitch's arms. It was probably said in the heat of the moment, and, as she recalled, there had been many of those.

Aunt Janice was in the kitchen already, and by the look of things, she'd made pancakes again, Dylan's favorite.

Dylan rushed to her, threw his arms around her legs. "Mommy won't let me stay with you, Aunt Janice!" he wailed.

With a quick look in Riley's direction, Aunt Janice picked him up. "Well, now, you're such a big boy, you can't cry now. Come on, I've made pancakes."

"Can I have mine with syrup?" He sniffled, the tears having miraculously disappeared.

"Of course, you may." Aunt Janice smiled and pulled a chair out for Dylan.

Only when Dylan was happily eating his pancakes did Aunt Janice move closer to Riley. "You do know he's more than welcome to stay with me."

But Riley was shaking her head even before her aunt had finished speaking. "I don't think I'll be back for Christmas this year, Aunt Janice. Maybe next year. I just have too much work."

"You've just demonstrated you can work from anywhere."

"I have to do the shoots at location…"

"I know. And during those times, Dylan could stay with me or Vivian and Aiden or Craig and Annie."

"My life… our life is back in Portland, Aunt Janice. Our home is there."

Aunt Janice patted Riley's hand. "Home is where the heart is, sweetheart, as both Craig and Aiden have come to realize. But I won't pester you again; I've said my piece. I just want to add this—life doesn't come with guarantees, my darling girl. You have to grab every chance of happiness you get; you never know how long you'll have it. I hope you have a good flight and, remember, I'm here if you need me."

Her phone rang. It was Annie. Again. When the phone rang again, Riley didn't even check; she put it on silent. It would be Vivian. Again.

Studiously ignoring her aunt's eyes, Riley turned away. "I'm taking the bags to the car."

Mitch would get up any minute now, and she wanted to be long gone before that happened. She didn't know what to say to Annie and Vivian. Once she and Dylan were back in Portland, she'd phone them. It would be a while, though, before she'd be ready to talk to Mitch.

MITCH WAS STILL dreaming about making love to Riley when his alarm went off. He opened his eyes, his heart stilled. She was gone. All the energy she'd brought with her had been sucked out of the room.

Sitting up slowly, he looked at the empty place beside

him. Hours ago, he'd still held her warm body close to him, kissed her; he'd made love to her. And she just got up and left? Not even a good-bye.

A big hole opened up inside of him. Cussing, he got up. She thought she could just up and leave without talking to him? They'd just have to see about that. Grabbing his phone, he dialed her number. She wasn't picking up. While texting her, he grabbed a shirt. How could she just leave?

Minutes later, he stopped in front of Janice's house. His heart dropped. The only car on the driveway was Janice's. Riley had already left.

As he jumped out of his car, the front door opened. Janice had her bag in her hand; she was on her way to school.

She waited for him next to her car.

"Is she—" he began but couldn't finish his question.

"They left a little while ago," she said. Pressing her fingers against her quivering lips, she looked away. "Poor Dylan didn't want to leave. I was hoping… but I suppose things between the two of you… um… just didn't work out."

"It worked out!" he cried out, running his fingers through his hair in frustration. "That's why I don't understand why she just left. When I woke up this morning, she was gone. I've tried to call her, I've texted her, but she is flat-out ignoring me. And after last night…" Realizing what he was admitting, he pressed his lips together. "I just don't understand. I was going to talk to her this morning, tell her

I… I…"

Janice dropped her hands, her eyes wide. "Tell her what?"

There was such a loud roaring in his ears, he couldn't think, let alone answer Janice.

"Mitch?"

"I… I have to go. See you at school." Without a backward glance, he stomped back to his car.

Riley had left. Even after they'd spent hours last night making love, she'd snuck out of his house without waking him up, without saying good-bye. She was going back to her life in Portland without a backward glance.

He'd been transported to a whole new universe while making love with her, but apparently, what had happened between them didn't mean that much to her.

He was going to have to forget about Riley.

Dropping his head on the steering wheel, he cussed softly. How the hell was he supposed to do that when every breath he took reminded him of her?

By eleven o'clock, Riley and Dylan were sitting in the plane, waiting to take off from Yellowstone airport in Bozeman.

Dylan had fallen asleep in his chair on the drive from Marietta, probably because of all the crying. She had nothing else to keep her thoughts busy but memories of her night with Mitch.

Every vivid detail kept replaying over and over in her mind—the way Mitch's eyes had darkened with desire, the way his hands had known exactly where and how to touch her, his breath in her ear, the broken words he'd whispered as he'd made love to her.

Made love. Her breath got stuck in her throat. What had happened between them had been so much more than sex. They'd made love. She'd made love because…

Her heart kicked against her ribs before it finally settled back in place.

Because she loved Mitch. Stunned, she leaned back in her seat. Against all logic, despite the high walls she'd erected around her heart, she'd gone and fallen in love with Mitch.

That was why she'd snuck out of his house this morning, why she hadn't answered his calls or reacted to his messages—she'd panicked because her heart had already known she'd fallen in love with him long before her mind had caught up. She couldn't talk to him without revealing how she felt about him.

At some point, she'd have to respond to his and to his sisters' calls, but not right now. Keeping herself from falling apart was using up all her energy at the moment.

"I don't wanna go home," Dylan said again, his bottom lip quivering. "What about Mike? He's my new friend. I like the school here. I don't wanna go home!"

Riley didn't know what to say. She couldn't tell her son she was running away, that she couldn't return to Marietta because she loved Mitch.

For him, this was probably a one-time thing—she'd learned the hard way that making love with someone didn't necessarily mean they felt the same way she did.

Trying to console Dylan, Riley felt like bursting into tears herself. She was doing the right thing. Hers and Dylan's lives were back in Portland. Her work was there. Okay, she could work from anywhere if she wanted to, but Marietta? Montana?

On top of everything else, yesterday morning's headache was back as well as an irritating scratching in the back of her throat. She'd taken Tylenol before they'd left Marietta, but this time the irritation refused to go away. Instead, the drumming behind her eyes was increasing by the minute. The last thing she needed now was to get the flu.

"Can't we get off the plane, Mommy?" Dylan sniffled. "I don't wanna go back!"

"Oh, sweetie, I have to go to work tomorrow."

"I could've stayed with Aunt Janice," he cried.

Fortunately, at that point, the air hostess called everyone's attention, and minutes later, the plane was in the air. Fascinated, Dylan looked down on the scenery below them, his anger at his mother forgotten for the moment. Leaning forward, she pointed out the beautiful Bridger range of mountains to him, trying very hard not to burst into tears.

Without her realizing it, the wide-open spaces, the beautiful mountain ranges of Montana, had crept into her heart. She had, in fact, also fallen in love with Marietta, Montana.

Swallowing against the lump and scratchiness in her throat, she leaned back and closed her eyes. Life wasn't always fair, as she'd learned when her dad and soon after her mom had died when she'd still needed them so much.

She'd made a home for her and Dylan in Portland. They just needed to be back where they belonged. Things would improve when they were back in their familiar environment.

VIVIAN AND ANNIE were waiting for Mitch on the porch of his house when he arrived back home on Friday.

Annie had a basket with her, as always, and Vivian a bottle of wine in her hand. For a moment, he wanted to turn around and drive away. With a sigh, he parked and got out. Best to get the whole inquisition over with as soon as possible. His sisters interfered in his life as he had interfered in theirs. It was what families did. What his did anyway.

"Hi, Mitch," Vivian said as he reached them. "I've brought wine."

"And I've made tapas." Annie smiled.

Unlocking his front door, Mitch shook his head. "Riley is gone. It's no surprise. We've known all along she was going to leave. I don't have anything to add."

"Oh, come on, that's not true," Vivian said as she moved into his house. "Aunt Janice said you invited Riley for a drink last night... Oh..." She pointed toward the two clean glasses and bottle of wine still standing on the coffee table where he'd put them last night. "So, she wasn't here?"

Annie took a platter out of her basket. "Let's sit down and have a glass of wine."

Putting his hands in his pockets, Mitch moved toward the window. Where his heart was supposed to be was a big hole. How the hell was he expected to simply forget what had happened between him and Riley and move on?

Although he'd never had a serious relationship, he'd dated, he'd had sex with women, but the intensity of his and Riley's lovemaking wasn't something he'd ever experienced before.

"Mitch?" Vivian's voice finally penetrated his thoughts.

With a sigh, he joined them.

Vivian handed him a glass of wine. "Let's begin at the start. What happened last night after we left you at the lake?"

"You do know that what happens in my life has nothing to do with any of you?" he tried.

Annie smiled. "Sorry, you broke that rule, if there was one, when you interfered in our love lives. Come on, spill."

Staring down into his wine, he nodded. "Okay, yes, Riley was here. And we... spent the night together. When I woke up this morning, though, she was gone. Didn't say good-bye, didn't leave a note or text. By the time I got to

Janice's house, she and Dylan had already left. She's not answering my calls, and she's ignoring my texts. I get the message loud and clear—she doesn't want to have anything to do with me."

"She also hasn't responded to our texts," Vivian said, frowning. "But surely something must have happened that upset her or…" Her frown cleared. Chuckling, she looked at Annie. "Do you think…"

Smiling, Annie nodded. "You know, you may just be right."

Mitch frowned. His sisters were doing that thing again where they used ordinary English words, but he didn't understand a word they were saying. "What are you talking about?"

"You had a good time last night?" Annie asked.

"Yes, we had—that's why…"

"And did you tell her how you feel about her?" Vivian asked.

Irritated, he crossed his arms. "What do you mean? We didn't really talk…"

Annie nodded and threw her arm in the air. "Ahh, now it all makes sense. You slept with her, and you didn't tell her you were hopelessly in love with her?"

"I don't understand…" he began before Annie's words registered. "You mean…" The roaring in his ears was back, and his heart was beating at an alarming rate. A firm band across his chest was tightening by the second, making breathing impossible. He jumped up, inhaled deeply. "Don't be ridiculous. I can't be in... What I mean is, we've basically just met. There is a connection, I'll give you that, but it's not as if I..." Inhaling deeply, he vehemently shook his head.

Vivian angled her head. "You notice how he struggles to say the L-word, Annie?"

Annie nodded. "I do. Strange that, don't you think? He lights up when he sees her, he keeps kissing her and touching her, but they just have a... what's the word he used?"

"Connection," Vivian said, straight-faced. "Whatever could he mean by that? Maybe," Vivian said, getting up, "you should go and reread your manuscript. Especially those parts describing Dorothy. Come on, Annie, he probably needs time to digest. He's a man, after all, and it takes them a bit longer to connect the dots."

Fed up, he stared at his sisters. "What freaking dots are you talking about?"

Annie got up and gave him a hug. "You'll figure it out. The heart wants what the heart wants."

Long after his sisters had left, he still stood at the window, looking outside. When he finally turned back, his eyes fell on the spot on his carpet where he and Riley had made love.

Closing his eyes, he could recall every moment he'd spent with her in his arms. The way she'd shuddered, the way she'd cried out his name, the way she'd brokenly sobbed when she'd reached a peak. And there had been several of those moments, he recalled.

Sighing, he headed for his room. He wasn't hungry; he wasn't going to sleep, so he might as well continue editing his story while he tried to figure out what this emptiness inside him meant.

Chapter Fifteen

FRIDAY, TWO WEEKS later, Riley was in front of her laptop, rubbing her temple. The scratchy throat and headache she'd had when she and Dylan had arrived back from Marietta was back, worse than before. Her whole body ached.

She'd felt slightly better over the past weekend, but then she'd made the mistake of taking Dylan to the park. It started to rain while they were there. She'd taken off her jacket to protect Dylan with the result she'd been icy cold and wet by the time they'd made it back home.

Her whole body was shaking, and she probably had a fever, as well. At some point, she should go and see the doctor as none of the over-the-counter meds she'd tried so far were helping, but a doctor's visit would have to wait for next week. She had way too much to do.

Her main concern at the moment was Dylan. He'd stopped crying when she dropped him off at school in the morning, and he didn't even complain about the school anymore, but he was clearly unhappy. The dejected little figure she picked up after school every day was breaking her heart. Even at home, he was listless. Her happy, laughing son had disappeared. She'd really hoped by now he would've made friends, but whatever the problem was, it wasn't going to go away miraculously; she'd have to go and talk to the teacher at some point.

She'd been so busy since their return and would probably have to work straight through the weekend to finish editing the pictures from this week's photo shoots.

Ugh, if this blasted headache would just disappear, she might be able to concentrate on her work. With a sigh, she took two more Tylenols and opened her emails. The tablets would hopefully ease her painful throat and help to bring down her fever.

She wasn't looking forward to today's photo shoot. Apart from the fact that the magazine wanted the shoot on Alberta Street, a busy part in the Arts District of the city, which meant there would be lots of people, it was also bitterly cold. The weather prediction was snow—usually a wonderful backdrop for a photo shoot but not when she was feeling so lousy.

Her eyes scanned her emails. Two emails were from magazines asking her to do photo shoots for their Valentine's Day edition. It wasn't even Christmas yet, for goodness' sake. She needed to stay busy, though, and responded quickly.

Clearing her sore throat, she opened the next email. And froze. It was from Mitch.

Dear Riley,

You left without saying goodbye. I'm trying to figure out why. I'm also trying to figure out why I can't forget a single moment of the night we spent together, why you're on my mind every waking moment, and that when I fall asleep, there you are, as well.

I assume you disappearing like that means you don't want to talk to or see me again. I have one request, though: please read my manuscript?

Waiting for you,
Mitch

By the time she'd finished reading the short note, there was a lump in her throat the size of a golf ball.

Dropping her aching head in her hands, she closed her eyes. She missed Mitch with every cell in her body. *It will be better after a week,* she'd tried to console herself with during those first two long nights, but after fourteen days and fourteen nights, he was still taking center stage in her mind. She had to accept it now; loving Mitch wasn't going to change. Ever.

Okay, she would read his story. Maybe once she'd done that, it would be easier to live with this constant emptiness inside her.

THE MOMENT HE got home on Friday evening, Mitch

walked up the stairs and opened his emails. Minutes later, he jumped up and started pacing. Riley had seen his email, he could see that, but she hadn't responded. Was she going to read his manuscript or was she simply going to ignore it like she'd been ignoring all his calls and texts?

Why was it bothering him so much? Why couldn't he stop thinking about her, dreaming about her, wanting her with every breath he took? Damn it, it had been two weeks.

Sighing, he opened his manuscript. He had no appetite, and he wasn't sleeping; he might as well finish the damn thing and send it to a publisher. Over the last few weeks, he'd scoured the internet, phoned people he knew in the publishing business, and at least he now had a few names of publishers and agents he could try.

Everyone he'd contacted had been quick to tell him not to expect a reaction soon. It could take months, even years before his book would be published. There was the self-publishing route he could take, of course, but he'd do that when he'd exhausted all the other options.

Craig, Annie's husband, was in marketing and had offered to help him with the promotion of the book, but that could only happen once he'd found someone willing to publish Dorothy and Joshua's story.

Mitch started on the first page. The words he'd used to describe Dorothy—long, fiery-red tresses, startling blue eyes, saucy smile—caught his eye as they did every time he read the first paragraph. He continued reading for another few pages before he stopped. His eyes were taking in the words, but his mind was still on the first chapter.

He scrolled back, read the words describing Dorothy again. The red hair, the slender body, the saucy smile. For a moment, he saw Riley so clearly in front of him, his head reeled.

Jumping up, he started pacing while images of Dorothy and Riley took turns appearing in front of him. His heart was galloping away at an alarming rate, his blood roaring in his ears. Riley, Riley. Riley.

Finally, as if in slow motion, the roaring subsided, and his heartbeat slowed down. Piece by piece, a messy puzzle came together until he understood why he'd been so crazy since Riley had left—he loved her; he was in love with her. Hopelessly. Of course.

Combing his fingers through his hair, he barked out a laugh. Why the hell had it taken him so long to realize this? Damn it, his sisters had known it long before he'd caught on. He'd been waiting for her since... since forever. The moment she'd arrived in Marietta, his life had begun to make sense.

He had to get to Riley. Right now. Her address? He didn't have her address. Cussing, he took out his phone. How could you love someone and not know where they lived? He phoned Annie; Vivian was probably still working.

His sister answered on the first ring. "Mitch?"

"I love her."

Annie laughed, not bothering to ask what he was talking about as she knew. "Of course, you do! I just don't know why it has taken you so long to figure it out."

"I have to go and see her. But… her address?"

Annie laughed. "You have it bad, don't you? Okay, this is what you have to do—go pack a bag—I'll make your reservation, and I'll text you her address. And Mitch?"

"Yeah?"

"Don't mess this up, okay?"

"I'll do my best."

"Riley… she's been hurt, as you know. Like us, she's also lost people she loved. She's rebuilt her life, and in her mind, she's created the perfect home for her and Dylan. Understandably, she's afraid of commitment, afraid to lose her identity when she allows someone else into her life. And she has Dylan to think of. You'll have to keep all of the above in mind when you see her. Still want to go to her?"

"Hell, yeah. I love her. I love Dylan. I want to be with them."

"Are you willing to move to Portland? Because she may not be prepared to leave her work and life."

"I want to be with her. Whatever it takes."

Annie sniffed. "Right answer. Go pack. I'll tell Vivian. I'll send you the boarding pass!"

"Thanks!" Mitch inhaled deeply. He was going to see Riley. Grabbing his overnight bag, he threw in a pair of jeans and a couple of shirts before he stopped.

An overnight bag was not going to work this time.

Annie phoned. There wasn't a flight tonight that could take him to Portland; the first one was the only one the next morning. Damn. But okay, now he had the time to pack properly. Afterward, he'd try to finish editing his manuscript.

RILEY HUDDLED IN her jacket as she walked toward Dylan's school. She was shivering, she was cold, and felt lousy.

After today's interminable shoot, she'd stopped at the doctor. Although she was feeling even worse than this morning, her throat was still on fire, and she had a splitting headache, she now had meds. All she wanted to do was get into bed and sleep until she felt better. She should stay in bed for two days, the smiling doctor had advised. If only… On a day like this one, she wished Aunt Janice or Craig or Aiden were close by… Or Mitch. He would've been such a great help…

Inhaling deeply, she lengthened her strides. To cry over what-ifs wasn't going to help anyone.

Dylan's teacher wanted to talk to her, not something she was looking forward to. She had no idea what was going on or whether she'd know how to handle the situation.

Riley knocked on the classroom door and opened it. A grim-looking teacher invited her in. Another boy, taller and bigger than Dylan, was standing next to a man, presumably his father. Dylan jumped up when he saw Riley and rushed into her arms. Picking him up, she hugged him close. His whole body was shivering. Burying his face in her neck, he clung to her.

"What seems to be the problem?" Riley asked.

The teacher introduced Riley to George and his father Paul before she turned to Riley. "Dylan hit George."

Riley's head was spinning. "Dylan? But he's half George's size…"

"I saw what happened," the teacher said, pressing her lips together.

"Dylan would never…"

"Well, he did," the dad chipped in, his face getting red. "I won't tolerate—"

Riley tried to focus on what the man was saying, but she was so cold, her headache so fierce, she only caught a word here and there.

"Unruly… expel… my poor boy…"

Inhaling deeply, she hitched Dylan higher on her hip. "I'm leaving," she told the teacher, ignoring Paul or Peter or whatever the man's name was. "And Dylan won't be coming back."

The teacher was still stuttering when Riley closed the door behind her.

Dylan pulled away, his eyes wet with tears. "I don't have to go back?"

She shook her head. "No, but we have to talk. Did you

hit George?"

"Yes, but he pushed Sadie and she fell."

"It doesn't matter what George did; you don't ever go around hitting people. You tell the teacher or you tell me, but you're not to hit anyone ever again. Hug them, help them, but we never hurt other people, okay."

"I'm sorry, Mommy," he sniffled. "I wanna go back to Aunt Janice's school."

Her headache pounding mercilessly behind her eyes, Riley hugged Dylan. "Oh, sweetie, I know, but we don't always get what we want, you know? You'll have to learn to accept that. Let's go home. I'll order pizza. How does that sound?"

BY SIX O'CLOCK Saturday morning, Mitch had pressed the send button. His manuscript was traveling through cyberspace, and it was out of his hands.

Relieved, he checked his watch. There was enough time to shower and put on a clean shirt before he had to leave for the airport.

Jumping up, he stretched his stiff muscles. He was excited, nervous, scared—all at the same time. What if he messed this up? What if Riley wasn't interested in anything he had to say?

In between his editing, these questions had been driving him insane. Numerous times he'd picked up his phone only to drop it again. She hadn't reacted to text before, so it would be senseless to send another one.

He hauled the big suitcase down the stairs and out onto the porch. Without a backward glance, he locked the door behind him.

As he turned around, a movement from the direction of his car drew his attention. Craig and Aiden were leaning against his car. Damn it to hell, he seriously didn't want to have to deal with the brother and the cousin right now. But, okay, he'd given them a hard time before he'd known they were serious about his sisters. He understood the protectiveness they were feeling. Didn't mean he liked it, though.

"Craig, Aiden." Unlocking his car, he heaved the suitcase into the trunk of the car.

With an eye on his luggage, Aiden cleared his throat. "You planning on a long trip?"

"Depends."

Craig stepped closer. "On what?"

"On whether Riley allows me to stay."

Aiden and Craig shared a look.

"You mean you'll be prepared to stay with her in Portland?"

"If she'll have me, I'm happy to stay anywhere, as long as she and Dylan are with me."

Aiden joined his cousin. "Why?"

"Because I love her."

For a fraction of a second, it was quiet before the cousins

grinned.

"Took you long enough." Aiden chuckled.

Mitch opened the door. "Yeah, well. As I recall, both of you also needed a push."

Craig's smile faded. "You hurt her you'll have to deal with us."

"I know."

"What about your job? Your house?" Aiden asked.

Mitch shrugged. "I'll be back on Monday. What happens after that will depend on what Riley wants."

Chapter Sixteen

RILEY WAS BURNING up. She was struggling to breathe, the simple movement of trying to lift her head, agony. What time was it? Where was Dylan?

"Mo-om?" Dylan's voice penetrated the fogginess surrounding her.

"Sweetie," she got out, but her throat was so sore, it was an effort to speak.

"You sound funny, Mommy. I'm hungry."

"Dylan. Where's Mommy's phone?" She tried to think who she could call, but her foggy brain could only come up with one name—Mitch. She'd call Mitch.

"Here's your phone, Mommy." He put it in her hands.

Riley tried to open her eyes, but the throbbing headache was making it difficult. Squinting, she found her contacts. Mitch. She had to call him. He'd know what to do. Where was his name? There it was. Trying to concentrate, she pushed the button, but the effort to hold onto the phone was too much, it slipped out of her hand.

Maybe Dylan could talk to him. She tried to lift her head, but with a groan, she leaned back again. "Talk to…

Mitch ..." Closing her eyes, she succumbed to the blackness that had been pulling at her since she'd woken up.

THE MOMENT THE plane landed in Portland's international airport, Mitch had his phone in his hand. He had Riley's address; he just needed to get an Uber to take him to her. Irritated, he waited. Why was it taking so long for the passengers to disembark?

Finally, it was his turn, and he quickly jogged down the stairs, taking in the impressive airport building. He'd read somewhere that the building was under construction and not yet finished.

As he followed the other passengers to collect his huge suitcase, his phone rang. He stopped in his tracks. Riley was calling him. Someone bumped into him from behind, swore, but he only registered it vaguely.

"Riley?" he asked as he moved to the side.

"Uncle Mitch?" the soft voice on the other side of the phone wasn't Riley but Dylan.

"Dylan? Is everything okay? Where's your mom?"

"In her bed. She doesn't open her eyes. I'm hungry."

Ice-cold fingers squeezed Mitch's throat until he was struggling to breath. "Is Mommy sleeping?"

"I don't know. She's not talking. I'm scared."

Frantically, Mitch looked around him. It was going to

take forever to get his luggage and then an Uber. He'd phone Craig or Aiden. Surely one of them would know someone close to Riley's house who could check on her.

"Dylan? You know what? I'm actually on my way to see you and your mom. Will you stay with her until I get there? I'm going to get us something to eat, as well, okay? You're such a big boy; I'm so proud of you."

"'Kay." Dylan sighed. "But hurry, Uncle Mitch. I'm really, really hungry."

"Promise. You sit tight; I'm on my way."

Dialing Annie's number, Mitch searched for directions to the baggage carousel. There it was. As he started running, Annie answered the phone.

SHE HAD TO open her eyes. Dylan needed her. Struggling against the layers of black fog surrounding her, Riley tried to speak, but her throat was so sore, the only sound she managed was a croak.

"It's okay, Mommy. Mitch is on his way. He's bringing food."

Was that her little boy? Putting out a hand, Riley tried to touch Dylan, but she couldn't reach him, her arms too heavy.

Had he said Mitch's name? Mitch was in Marietta; he couldn't be here. He probably never wanted to talk to her again. She had to get up and make something for Dylan to eat. Maybe if she lay quietly for another few minutes, she'd feel better.

The black fog pulled her in again.

TRAFFIC WAS SLOW, and they were barely moving. Frustration, worry, and fear were all gnawing at Mitch's gut. Annie had said Craig had the number of the neighbor across the street from Riley. He was going to ask her to pop in at Riley's house to make sure she was okay, but he hadn't heard from his sister again.

According to the GPS on his phone, they were ten minutes away from Riley's house, but at this speed, it could take another half an hour.

"Is there perhaps a quicker route?" he finally asked. "It's urgent I get to my destination as soon as possible."

The driver glanced his way. "More the hurry, more the obstacles. We'll get there."

Swallowing his irritation, Mitch looked down at his phone. The Uber driver had been sharing his lines of wisdom since he'd picked up Mitch, but right now, he didn't want to hear another one. His only concern was to get to Riley and Dylan as soon as possible.

He could try to phone Riley again, but he didn't want to upset Dylan further. He'd text Annie to find out whether she'd spoken to her brother and cousin.

As he opened his texts, Riley's name was at the top. Frowning, he checked the time. The message had been sent after he'd spoken with Dylan. Did it mean…

Quickly, he opened the message.

I haven't stopped thinking about the kiss either. You stirred up forgotten feelings. I have no idea how not to think about you.

It took him another few seconds to understand what he was reading—it had to be the text Riley had told him about, the one she'd written in response to his very first text to her, the one she'd never sent.

He reread the text over and over until he knew the words by heart. Why the hell hadn't she sent it to him? Why hadn't she told him? Was she okay? Why had he wasted so much time before he'd known he loved her? Why…

"We're here."

Still stunned, Mitch looked at the driver, not immediately registering what he'd said.

The guy pointed toward the house. "We're here."

"Oh. Okay, thanks."

Chuckling, the driver got out of his car to open the trunk. "You have a woman on your mind?"

Mitch took his luggage from the man, his eyes on the front door. Was it his imagination or was the door open?

"Thanks," he said, and grabbing the suitcase, he rushed toward the front door.

As he approached, an older woman opened the door wider. She had Dylan's hand in hers. "You must be Mitch?"

"Uncle Mitch!" Dylan cried and ran toward Mitch. He dropped his luggage and picked up the little boy.

"Hello, big guy. How is your mom?"

"Still sleeping. But I've had pizza."

"Were you the one who ordered the pizza?" the woman asked. "I'm Sally, by the way. Neighbor across the street. Craig phoned me to ask if I'd check in on Riley. He knocked on my door and introduced himself earlier this year when he'd visited Riley."

"Where is she?"

"Still sleeping and feverish. I was just about to help her into clean pajamas when I saw the car dropping you off."

"I'm here now. Thank you for your help," Mitch said.

The woman looked at Dylan before she spoke to him again. "You're sure you can manage?"

"I'm sure. Thanks again for stepping in. We appreciate it."

Mitch closed the door after the woman. "So where is your mom sleeping?" he asked Dylan as he put him down.

"Come, I'll show you."

Riley was moving restlessly in her bed, tangled up in the sheets. Her face was as white as the sheets she was laying on, making the freckles on her nose and face more prominent. Mitch placed a hand on her forehead. She was burning up.

Trying to stay calm, he took Dylan's hand. "I'm going to help your mom. Want to watch some television?"

Dylan's eyes widened. "I'm not s'posed to watch during

the day, Mommy says."

"Sometimes it's okay. Today is one of those times. Come on, let's get you settled."

Minutes later, Mitch was back in Riley's room. Dylan was watching a children's story, and with any luck, he'd be happy for a while.

Sitting down next to Riley on the bed, Mitch combed her hair out of her face. "Riley, sweetheart…"

Her eyes fluttered open. "Mitch. Must be dreaming. Mitch… in Marietta."

"I'm here. For as long as you want me, I'll be here. How do I get hold of your doctor?"

Her eyes closed again. "Saw him. Meds somewhere." Her words were a mere whisper, but because his head was bent over her, he'd heard her.

Meds. Somewhere. Where would she have put it? He got up and looked around. A brown paper bag on her dresser caught his attention. Opening it, he took the contents out. He had no idea what the different tablets were, but fortunately, Vivian would know. Dialing his sister's number, he sat down next to Riley again and picked up her hand.

CAUTIOUSLY, RILEY OPENED her eyes. The pounding behind her eyes had subsided, and she could swallow without wanting to cry.

As she turned, a strange sound penetrated her fuzzy mind. She froze. What was that? Very slowly, she moved her head. What on earth? She inhaled sharply.

Sitting in a chair next to her bed, his head resting against the back, was Mitch. The sound she'd heard was his soft snoring. As she stared at him, foggy images appeared: Mitch washing her with infinite tenderness, Mitch dressing her, Mitch cuddling her, wiping her face, urging her to drink her meds, feeding her soup. Mitch.

Slowly, she moved up against the pillows.

Mitch opened his eyes, and when he saw her watching him, he quickly got up. "Riley, sweetheart… can you hear me?" Big hands slid down her arms, cupped her face. "How are you feeling?"

"Like a few hundred buffalos trampled over me."

Clearly relieved, he tugged her closer to him. "I've been so worried about you. You took the meds, but your fever wouldn't let up. Vivian said if it's not better by morning, I should take you to the hospital." He put a hand to her forehead. "You're not feverish anymore, thank goodness."

Frowning, she stared at him. "Why are you here? With me? In Portland?"

Smiling, he combed her hair out of her face. "Dylan phoned me, but I was already in Portland. We'll talk later, but only after you're feeling better."

Swinging her legs over the side of the bed, Riley tried to stand up. Mitch moved closer. "Bathroom…" As she got up, though, the whole room tilted, and she grabbed onto him to stay upright.

He put an arm around her as they moved toward the bathroom. "Slowly. You've barely eaten the last two days…"

"What do you mean two days? What day is it?"

"It's Sunday night…" He checked his watch. "Nearly midnight."

"Sunday night? But that can't be. I fetched Dylan from school this morning…"

"That would be Friday morning, two days ago."

"And you've been here the whole time?"

He opened the bathroom door. "Since yesterday lunchtime. Do you need help again…"

"What do you mean again?"

"You could barely stand, let alone go to the bathroom on your own."

Blushing, she inhaled. "You mean you…"

"Someone had to do it." He was the picture of innocence. "I was here."

"Well, I'm fine now, thank you." And with as much dignity as she could muster under the circumstances, she closed the door behind her.

His low chuckle followed her all the way to the mirror. Horrified, she touched her face. Look at her—hair all over the place, pale as a ghost, all you could see were freckles. Groaning, she took off her pajamas and got into the shower.

As the water cascaded over her, she remembered big

hands washing her, drying her, clothing her…

Why was Mitch here?

As she picked up the towel after her shower, she noticed the clean pair of pajamas on the small counter. Mitch. Which meant he'd entered the bathroom while she'd been in the shower.

There was a knock on the bathroom door. "Are you okay?" Mitch called.

"I'm fine." Quickly she rubbed herself dry and put on the clean pajamas. By the time she was finished, she was exhausted. She wasn't sure she'd make it to the bed, and her hair was still wet.

"I'm coming in," Mitch announced before he opened the door. He gave her one look. Before she realized what he was going to do, he'd picked her up. "Why didn't you call me? You're white as a sheet again."

With long strides, he carried her back to her bed. As he put her down, she saw he'd stripped the bed and made it again with fresh sheets.

Frowning, she glared at him. "I can make my own bed, you know."

"I know. But I'm here, you're ill, so I've made it for you."

"Why are you here, Mitch?"

Ignoring her question, he pulled the sheets over her. "Let's dry your hair, and then I'll make something for you to eat. You've barely eaten over the last few days. What would you like? Toast and egg? Omelet? I've bought some tins of soup?" Walking to her dresser, he fetched the hairdryer and a brush. After plugging it in, he sat next to her, turning her shoulders so that he was behind her.

"I can dry my own hair." She was cross and wanted to cry.

"You're an independent woman, got it. At the moment, though, you need help. So tell me what you'd like to eat."

"It's okay. I'll get something in the morning…"

Ignoring her, he combed out her hair with infinite patience before he switched on the hairdryer.

Closing her eyes, she tried to keep upright, but she was so tired, her body slumped forward. Pulling her back against him, Mitch continued drying her hair. Leaning against his chest, she finally relaxed. She was feeling too poorly at the moment to argue with him, but she'd give him a piece of her mind when she was feeling better.

By the time he'd finished, she was just about asleep. Removing his arms from her, he moved her back against the pillows. "Come on, sweetheart, tell me what you want to eat?"

"It's really not necessary…"

Bending down quickly, he kissed her. His lips were warm, trying to tell her something, but before she could figure out what, he was heading out of the room. "If you can't decide, I'll decide for you."

Chapter Seventeen

WHEN MITCH NEXT opened his eyes, it was broad daylight. He'd been sleep deprived when he'd arrived in Portland on Saturday, and over the last twenty-four hours, he hadn't had much sleep either.

Riley. Dylan. He'd told Dylan to wake him up when he was still sleeping so what happened this morning?

Jumping out of bed, he headed toward Dylan's room. Halfway down the corridor, though, he heard voices from the direction of the kitchen. Dylan and Riley.

She was dressed and standing in front of the stove. Dylan was sitting at the counter when he walked in.

"Uncle Mitch!" Dylan cried out, and climbing off his chair, he rushed toward Mitch. "Mommy isn't sleeping anymore; she's making pancakes."

Mitch picked up the little boy and hugged him before he helped him back on his chair. "I can see that."

Moving closer to her, his eyes slid over her. She was still way too pale, but at least there was a glimmer of a blush on her cheeks.

He touched her face. "Hi, how are you feeling?"

"Better, thanks. Shouldn't you be teaching at the high school in Marietta, Montana?" Her eyes slid over his chest. "With a shirt on?"

Bending down, he kissed her. He hadn't planned it, but there was no way he could be this close to her and not touch her. And when he touched her, he had to kiss her.

Her eyes were bright blue by the time he lifted his head. "I spoke to the principal yesterday."

"But I'm fine now—you should go back."

"Not before we talk."

"So talk."

"We'll talk tonight when Dylan's asleep." He lowered his voice. "From what he's dropped here and there, I gather he's not attending school anymore?"

Groaning, she slid the batch of pancakes on to a plate. "Don't remind me. I'll have to find him another school, and it's not that easy to get a good one that's not too far from our house. You can have a pancake when you've put a shirt on."

"Won't you be tempted to get rid of it again?" he couldn't help teasing.

She turned her back on him but not before he'd seen the flush creeping up her neck.

"Okay, I'll go get dressed. Oh, by the way, thanks for the text. A pity you didn't send it two months ago. It would've saved us both so much time." Putting his hands on her shoulders, he dropped a kiss on her head before he headed toward the room where he'd put his stuff.

As soon as Mitch had left the kitchen, Riley grabbed her phone. And lo and behold, the message she'd written to Mitch, right after her return from Craig and Annie's wedding, had been sent.

But how... Flashes of what had happened on Friday came back to her. She'd tried to call Mitch, she remembered. Even in her delirious state, he'd been the one she'd reached out to. Damn it, this love thing was making her do stupid things...

Mitch entered again, this time in a shirt, the denim one he looked so good in; she had trouble not staring at him. Today, the blue eye was nearly navy, the brown one just about black—exactly the way they were when she and Mitch had made love.

She and Mitch making love was so not something she should be thinking about. Inhaling, she grabbed the pan and turned her back on Mitch. "I... I shouldn't have sent the message, please forget about it."

"Riley..."

"And thank you for phoning Annie. Apparently, Craig then called Sally to come and look after Dylan. Everyone back in Marietta called this morning. Thank you for your help, but I'm fine now. You really don't have to stay."

Mitch chuckled. "Riley, sweetheart, there are more than enough pancakes for all of us. Why don't you sit down and join us?"

Her phone rang. Thank goodness. If she had to sit near Mitch, she might just begin to drool.

"Excuse me." Heading out of the kitchen, she answered the call.

Minutes later, still stunned, she walked back into the kitchen.

"Riley?" Mitch said, frowning. "Everything okay?"

She nodded, her head spinning. "I am. It's just... the phone call? It was a gallery in Bozeman. They'd contacted me earlier this year about an exhibition over Christmas, one where photographers all over the country would showcase their work. I declined at the time, but now one of the artists has apparently dropped out and they want to know if I have something they could use. This Friday. They need two or three photographs, the rest—the enlargement, framing—they'll do in Bozeman."

"And? What did you say?"

"I'll have to think about it. I don't really do portrait studies. I focus on the clothes, the fashion, not the faces."

"Your work is amazing, Riley—go for it."

"I don't know if I have something…" Staring at Mitch, an idea popped into her mind. What if… No, that was ridiculous; she could never do that.

Gathering his and Dylan's plates, Mitch got up. "Why don't you take your laptop and go back to bed. Dylan and I will clean up here before we head out to the park I saw nearby. We'll also pick up some steaks I can grill tonight."

"It's really not necessary. You have to go back to Marietta…"

He walked closer, picked up her hand. "I'm here now. Let me help?"

IT WAS NINE o'clock in the evening before Dylan finally fell asleep. Mitch softly closed the bedroom door behind him. Yawning, he turned around. He'd nearly fallen asleep himself, but he had to speak to Riley.

He stopped in his tracks. Riley was standing in the door of the room he'd been using since his arrival. She was looking at something inside the room, a slight frown on her forehead.

He advanced slowly. "Something the matter?"

"Is that your suitcase?"

Nodding, he took her hand. "I was hoping to move into your room, but since you were ill, I've moved in here. Temporarily, I hope."

Troubled eyes stared at him. "I don't understand."

"Let's sit down…"

She pulled her hand from his. "I don't want to sit down; I want to know why you are here, why you've brought a suitcase the size of a small room, and why you've looked after me."

"All good questions and ones I'm happy to answer if you'll answer one question I have."

"Seriously, Mitch…"

"Just one."

Hands on hips, she glared at him. "Okay, ask away. I don't know whether I'll answer you, though."

Inhaling deeply, he took both her hands in his. "The message you sent me—do you mean what you said?"

"I don't even remember what I said—that was months ago!"

"Really? Because I remember every word. 'I haven't stopped thinking about the kiss; you stirred up forgotten feelings.' And my favorite part. 'I have no idea how not to think about you.' Did you mean all of that?"

With a sigh, her shoulders slumped forward. "Okay, yes, I meant it. I still do, but you're in Marietta. I'm here. I have Dylan to think about, and it's not as if you…" Swallowing, she looked away.

Cupping her face, he turned her face toward him again. "It's not as if I… what?"

She shook her head, her eyes bright with tears.

This was it. The moment of truth. Time to go for broke. "Because if you were going to say it's not as if I love you, you'd be wrong."

Those beautiful lavender-blue eyes stared at him. "What… what are you saying?"

"I love you. I'm in love with you, Riley O'Sullivan. And

I want to spend the rest of my life with you and Dylan if you'll have me. That's why I have the huge suitcase—I had to pack for forever, and winter jackets take up a lot of space, you know."

One emotion after the other darted across her face, until her eyes were wide with panic. Not quite the emotion he was hoping for. Even before she opened her mouth, his heart was falling to the ground, breaking into a thousand little pieces. She didn't feel the same way.

Dropping her hands, she stepped back. "This could never work, Mitch, you know that. This house… Portland, they are my sanctuary, our home. I can't leave here. And you can't stay here; your life, your family is in Marietta. Just please go."

Holding onto his temper took a lot of effort, but he tried. "Can we talk about it? Please?"

"Talking isn't going to change anything. I won't survive losing one more person I love."

He was turning away from her before her words penetrated his chaotic thoughts.

Frowning, he faced her again. "Repeat what you just said?"

"I don't want to talk about it!" she called out.

"Not that part. The part where you say you won't survive…"

"Losing one more person I—" Shocked blue eyes met his. She hadn't realized what she'd said.

"So, you do love me?"

"It doesn't matter, don't you see? Your life is in Marietta, mine is here. This is where I belong…"

"That's what you keep saying, but I think you know it hasn't been true for a while now."

"Of course, it's true. You don't know me; you don't know anything about me…"

He reached out and stroked her face. "I know everything about you. I know you love wearing flowy clothes; I know you love multicolored earrings; I know you love your son; I know you care deeply about your cousin and brother. I know you'll get on a plane, no matter what time of day, to fly across states to be with your aunt because you thought she was ill. I know you're an introvert, you like your own space, you don't like crowds. I also know the exact hue of blue your eyes get when you're aroused. I know the different sounds you make in your throat when we make love, and now I know you love me. I'm here because I don't ever want to be without you again. But if that's not what you want, I'll go."

She stared at him, her eyes filling with tears.

He rubbed his face. "You mean to tell me I've actually gone and spoiled it all by saying something stupid like I love you?"

"Mitch …" she whispered brokenly.

Not even his feeble attempt at a joke helped. "I refuse to let this end like this, I love you, damn it."

"Sometimes it's not enough…"

He was getting desperate. "We can make it work, I know we can."

"I have so much baggage, I don't know…"

"That's okay. I do know. I know we belong together, I know you're the one for me and I know we'll be good together—you, me and Dylan. We all have baggage, but it's easier if we carry it together."

"I… I need time, Mitch. I wasn't looking for this, and then I met you and my calm and quiet existence I've been working so hard to achieve has been blown to bits. I don't know whether I'm coming or going and I can't think straight when you're here with me. I… have to think this through."

Bewildered and disappointed, Mitch stared down at her. She loved him, but she kept throwing obstacles in the way.

Taking out his phone, he booked an Uber to pick him up. "You want time? Okay, I'll give you time, damn it. But I don't like it. You're not getting rid of me this easily. What is between us is not something that's going to disappear. You know that, don't you?"

She nodded, tears running down her cheeks.

With a sigh, he cupped her face and wiped the tears away with his thumbs. "We've made love, I've looked into these gorgeous blue eyes of yours. You love me, whether you're prepared to say it out loud or not. You never would've allowed me to touch you if you hadn't loved me."

"Mitch…"

"Okay, I'm going. For the moment. But I'm not giving

up on us. Not by a long shot."

⁂

LONG AFTER THE sound of the Uber that had picked up Mitch had faded, Riley was still standing in front of her window, watching the street.

Mitch loved her. He'd shown up here and nursed her back to normal while looking after Dylan. He bathed her, dressed her, cooked for her. He was everything she'd ever wanted in a man. So why did she send him away? What difference was time going to make?

Sniffling, she turned back to her bed. It didn't matter, though—there was no way a relationship between them could ever work.

Why not? A pesky little voice wanted to know.

Because… she couldn't lose someone again, because she'd spent every waking moment since she'd been dumped at the altar trying to get her life back on track and she was finally at a point where she had the home she'd been missing ever since their parents had died. Because she liked neat and tidy…

Yeah? Her life was never going to be neat and tidy ever again. She was always going to love Mitch, always going to miss him. But she'd build this home for her and Dylan…

Home? The little voice prodded. Or merely a house?

Because… she got under the duvet, turned on her side,

and hugged her knees close to her body.

Because she didn't think she was good enough. What if at some point Mitch realized, like Percy had, she wasn't really what he'd wanted?

Turning her face into her pillow, she cried.

***

EARLY THE NEXT morning, the ringing of her phone woke up Riley. Checking her watch, she groaned. It was barely six o'clock, and Dylan was still sleeping. She couldn't believe she'd actually fallen asleep the previous night, as she'd cried and cried until there hadn't been any tears left. Although her heart was aching, her headache was at least gone, and she was feeling much better physically. Emotionally, though, she was a mess.

It was a call from Annie. Damn it, she should've known. The whole freaking town of Marietta probably knew by now exactly what had happened between her and Mitch last night.

"Hi, Annie," she said cautiously.

"So it's true." Annie sighed. "I didn't want to believe Mitch. You don't want him to stay even though he's told you he loves you?"

"Oh, Annie, I have to think about the whole thing. What if I let him down somehow? When I work, I get lost in what I do. I burn food, I forget to buy groceries. Mitch could do so much better than me."

It was quiet for such a long time that Riley thought Annie had put the phone down.

She checked. "Annie? You still there?"

"What's that thing you do?" Annie finally asked. "Craig has told me about it. Something about looking at a person's face to see the kind of person he or she is?"

Sighing, Riley rolled her eyes. "Physiognomy?" What was Annie going on about?

"Yeah, that. What did you see on Mitch's face when he told you how he feels?"

"I… I don't know…" she began crossly before Annie's words sank in.

Mitch's face… It wasn't difficult to conjure up his features, to see his even, smooth brows, slanting eyes, slim nose, strong chin—all indicative of someone who was confident, had self-control, had a strong character—things she'd noticed before, but what she hadn't seen, hadn't wanted to see, to be exact, was the expression in his eyes last night.

She'd seen that look on every picture she'd taken of him, and she'd seen it when they'd made love. Mitch really loved her, and he wanted to be with her. That was what he'd said. That was what his face, his eyes had told her. What was more, he got her, he really understood her, and he loved her anyway, oddities and all. He knew the kinds of clothes she loved to wear, he knew how much her family meant to her, he'd figured out she was an introvert, and he knew exactly how to make love to her.

"He… loves me as I am," she whispered.

"Of course, he does. And could I just add—we've all fallen in love with you and Dylan. We're a family and families should be together."

Before Riley could answer, her bedroom door opened and Dylan stormed in. "Where is Mitch? He's not in his room? Mommy?" Dylan's lip quivered. "I want Mitch; where is Mitch?"

"Mitch has left, sweetie…"

To her utter dismay, Dylan burst into tears. "But he… he was supposed to be my Christmas m'racle. Aunt Janice said…" More tears rolled down his cheeks.

Christmas miracle? What was her little boy talking about?

"I'm here to help. Let me know if I can help with the Christmas miracle, okay?" Annie said before she ended the call.

Putting her phone down, Riley reached out to Dylan. "Come here, sweetie. What Christmas miracle are you talking about?"

"I wanted Uncle Mitch to be your husband, so that he can be my daddy. I even asked Santa! But now he's gone, and I won't get my Christmas m'racle." And sobbing, he leaned against Riley.

Her own eyes wet with tears, Riley hugged her little boy close. She remembered Dylan whispering to Aunt Janice his secret. So, getting Mitch for his dad was what he'd wanted.

"You know what?" she sniffled. "It's not Christmas yet."

Dylan sat up, tears forgotten. "You mean Mitch could still be your husband and my dad?"

Shaking her head, she laughed through her tears. "I don't think that will happen, sweetie, but maybe we could all live together in one house. I'll have to ask him."

Dylan's eyes widened. "In Marietta? So I can go to school with Aunt Janice? And we can go and skate? And… and…"

Swallowing back her tears, Riley hugged her son. "Not so fast. I'll have to talk to Uncle Mitch first. You see, I think I've hurt him…"

Inhaling sharply, Dylan stared at her. "Did you hit him? You said we're not s'posed to hurt other people!"

"I know, sweetie, I know. I'll have to apologize to him, I just don't know whether he'll accept my apology, but I'll try, I promise."

"He will," Dylan said. "I'll also tell him you're sorry."

Laughing through her tears, she gave him another hug before she jumped out of bed. "We have a lot of things to do. But first, there is a story I have to read, and then I have to call a few people. I'll make breakfast, and then you can tell me what you want to watch on television."

Dylan's eyes widened. "On a school day?"

"Sometimes it's okay."

Nodding, Dylan slid off the bed. "That's what Mitch

said."

"Really?"

By the time Dylan had finished telling her about everything Mitch had done, Riley was ready to get on the first plane to Marietta. But there were things to be done, people to phone.

Chapter Eighteen

MITCH GOT HOME late from school on Wednesday. He'd only arrived back late the day before as he couldn't get an earlier flight.

Schools were closing on Friday for the Christmas break, which meant he had the rest of today and tomorrow to make a plan to persuade Riley he really loved her. He'd been wracking his brain, trying to think what else he could tell her or do to persuade her he'd meant every word he'd said to her.

His phone rang as he walked into his house. It wasn't any of his contacts, but it could be a parent.

"Mitch Miller."

"Mr. Miller, my name is Paul Winters, I'm an editor at…"

Mitch sat down quickly. He knew exactly who Paul Winters was—a well-known editor at one of the major publishers. What he didn't know was why the guy was calling him.

"O'Sullivan phoned my wife. I was curious enough to read your manuscript."

"Um… O'Sullivan… sorry, I didn't quite catch what you were saying?" Rubbing his face, Mitch swallowed his groan. He sounded like a complete idiot.

"Riley O'Sullivan phoned my wife, Elana, about your manuscript. They've been friends since grade two or three, I forget exactly when. Anyway, I remember seeing your email, but we get so many submissions, I probably wouldn't have read yours before sometime next year. Fortunately, because Riley phoned, I have. Do you mind sending me the rest of the manuscript as soon as possible? At this point, I can't guarantee we'll publish your book, but I can tell you I like what I've read so far."

"Yeah… I mean, yes, thank you. Of course, I'll send it right away."

His head reeling, Mitch put his phone down after the editor had ended the call. Riley had phoned a friend about his manuscript? He had to call her, right now. Minutes later, though, he threw his phone down. She wasn't answering. Damn it, what was he going to do about her?

Paul wanted his manuscript. Racing up the stairs, he felt lighter, happier. Nothing was quite certain at this moment—not about Riley or his manuscript—but his future wasn't looking quite so bleak either.

His phone rang. It was Vivian.

"Hi, Viv," he said with a smile. "I've just sent the rest of my manuscript to a publisher. And apparently, I should thank Riley for the opportunity."

"Riley? I don't understand."

Laughing out loud, he told his sister what had just happened.

"Oh, Mitch, I'm so happy for you!" Vivian exclaimed when he'd finished. "I hope you've thanked Riley."

"She's not answering my calls, but I haven't given up hope."

"Well, while you're planning your next move, Annie and I have decided to treat you with a trip to Bozeman. Monday is Christmas, and we haven't done any shopping yet. We'll pick you up after school on Friday. Craig and Aiden will meet us in Bozeman. They're picking up Janice and would be leaving earlier."

Shaking his head, Mitch laughed. "It seems I don't really have a say in this?"

"Nope."

"Okay, fine. But the two of you will have to help me find a way to persuade Riley I meant it when I told her I loved her."

Vivian chuckled. "That's what sisters are for."

RILEY HAD NEVER been this nervous in her life before. For the umpteenth time, she checked her phone. No text or missed calls from any of her family members. She'd seen Mitch's call earlier, but she wasn't ready to talk to him just yet.

She smiled and greeted the guests as they arrived at the exhibition, but her eyes kept wandering to the door.

A sharp-looking Dylan was standing proudly at her side. Aunt Janice had taken them shopping this morning. Riley had tried her best to tell her aunt she really didn't need more clothes, but Aunt Janice on a mission was not easily stopped.

"Here you are," Aunt Janice said, out of breath. "Riley, sweetheart, your work... those portraits of Mitch... I'm blown away by your talent."

As Riley turned to greet her aunt, she couldn't help smiling. Nobody could ever mistake Aunt Janice for a wallflower. Dressed in red and animal print, bangles on her arms, a pair of red high heels complementing her outfit, Aunt Janice was anything but your typical godmother.

"Thanks, Aunt Janice. I couldn't have done what I do without your support."

"And look at you!" her aunt gushed. "I'm so glad you settled for this soft yellow dress. The high neckline in front with the lower back—it suits you perfectly. You look absolutely stunning."

"Thank you for buying it for me." Riley smiled. "It's a tad shorter than what I normally wear, but I feel good in it." What she didn't add was that she had to use all and any ammunition she had if she wanted another chance with Mitch.

"Someone is trying to get your attention," Aunt Janice

said. "I'll keep Dylan occupied; the others should be here shortly."

The owner of the gallery wanted to introduce Riley to more guests. She smiled and nodded, trying her best to appear interested in whatever they were saying. Hopefully nobody would ask her anything afterward. She could see their mouths moving but making sense of what they were actually saying wasn't possible. All her attention was on the entrance.

Mitch helped Annie out of Craig's car before he looked around him. Aiden had parked right behind them and both he and Annie joined them on the sidewalk. Apparently, they were meeting Janice later. "Where are we exactly? I don't see any restaurants on this block?"

Annie put her hand through his one arm, Vivian through the other. "The night is young, Mitch. There is something you have to see first." Annie smiled.

Warily, Mitch looked at his brothers-in-law for support. "What do I have to see?"

Both Aiden and Craig were grinning. "You may as well surrender."

It was only when they entered the venue that Mitch realized what it was. A gallery. His eyes searched the walls. Portraits.

"An exhibition of portraits," he muttered, his brain desperately trying to grasp something he should know.

"Indeed." Annie chuckled. "There are two, in particular, you need to see. Over here, come on."

As he followed his sisters, people turned and stared at him. Some nodded while others smiled. What the hell…

As his sisters dragged him farther into the gallery, his heart skidded to a stop, and a loud noise filled his ears, making it impossible to hear anything else. Against the wall, beautiful portraits were on display.

Portraits. Riley. His head reeling, he took a deep breath. She'd told him about a gallery in Bozeman that was interested in her work. They were looking for portraits, if he remembered correctly. Looking at one portrait study after the other hanging on the walls, he realized that this had to be the exhibition. With everything that had happened since, he hadn't given the phone call she'd received another thought, but she'd obviously decided to send them some of her work.

Things were finally beginning to make sense. That was why they were here. His sisters wanted to show him Riley's works. His heart kicked against his ribs—did that mean Riley was here? In Bozeman?

The next portrait stopped him in his tracks. He recognized it instantly. It was a picture of him, one of the many Riley had taken of him on Craig and Annie's wedding day, the ones she had saved under the folder SOMETHING STUPID on her laptop.

This particular one had been taken after he'd left the bride with her groom. He was walking back to take his seat. There was a smile on his face, but his eyes were filled with tears. The background was faded, the focus on the contrasting emotions on his face.

"Isn't it amazing how Riley has captured exactly who you are? My big brother with the big heart who has never been afraid or uncomfortable to cry in front of everyone. But come and look at this one—it's my favorite." Grabbing his hand, Vivian pulled him around the corner.

Another huge portrait of him hung against this wall. Dazed, he stepped back. It was a bit disconcerting looking at such a huge picture of oneself, but as he stared, the feeling faded.

Around him people were talking, and some were whispering. They'd obviously recognized him, but he ignored everything else and focused on the portrait.

Struggling to breathe, he tried to look critically at the work. He'd been looking directly at the camera, directly at Riley, when she'd clicked her camera. In awe, he noticed the perfect way she'd used light and background, the small smile around his mouth, but what stole his breath was the emotion in his eyes.

He hadn't even known it at the time, but her camera had picked it up. Look at that—he'd already been in love with her. It was there, in his eyes, for all to see.

As he stared at the huge portrait, he remembered the exact moment when Riley had taken this one. The remarkable thing was, this moment had been captured earlier in the day, long before he and Riley had danced together, long before he'd become aware of that first tug at his heartstrings.

Somehow, though, his heart had known she was the one for him, long before the rest of him had caught on.

Stunned, he turned around. The crowd parted, and a vision in soft yellow walked toward him. Riley. His heart sighed. She was here, and within moments he'd be able to touch her. She was holding Dylan's hand tightly in hers, her eyes on Mitch, those blue eyes telling him everything he'd wanted to know.

Without any message from his brain, his feet moved toward her.

Then Dylan saw him. "Uncle Mitch!" he cried as he dropped his mom's hand and rushed toward Mitch. "Mom, look—it's Uncle Mitch."

By this time, the rest of the crowd had figured out something was going on, and every eye in the room had turned in their direction.

Mitch bent to pick up Dylan, his eyes never leaving Riley.

"Uncle Mitch is here," Dylan told the crowd. "It's a Christmas miracle."

While everyone laughed, Mitch moved closer to where Riley was standing.

With her eyes never leaving his, she reached out a hand.

"You're here," she breathed as he took her hand.

"Of course. You should've told me."

"I wasn't sure you'd take my call."

"I'll always take your calls. You're the one who didn't answer my call yesterday."

"I wanted tonight to be a surprise. I wasn't sure whether I'd be able to keep the secret."

"I got a call from a publisher. Apparently, thanks to you?"

"You're not mad?"

"How can I be mad? You helped me. Thank you. He's asked for the rest of the manuscript—it may not have happened without your help."

"Of course, it would've—it's a beautiful story." A smile lit up her face. "I like your Dorothy. She also has red hair."

Chuckling, he moved closer, Dylan still in his arms. "My muse's hair is red. I had no choice. I love you, haven't I told you that?"

The crowd that had been watching them was finally moving away; something else had grabbed their attention.

"Mommy, you haven't said you're sorry," Dylan whispered before he turned to Mitch. "Mommy is sorry she hurt you. Can we now all live together in your house?"

"May we…" He knew Riley was correcting Dylan, but her eyes were on him.

"I'd really like that." He smiled, his heart just about jumping out of his body.

"Okay, you two," Craig interrupted, taking Dylan from Mitch and handing him his car keys. "We're taking Dylan back to Marietta, and he's staying with us for the night. Mitch, you know where I've parked. Drive safely." Pulling Riley closer, he kissed her forehead. "Good job, coz, we're so proud of you."

Annie hugged Riley and Mitch. "Breakfast at our place tomorrow morning. And prepare yourselves—we want details."

Aiden and Vivian were next to say their good-byes.

"You did good, sis," Aiden said, his voice not quite steady. "Mom and Dad… they would've been so proud of you."

Sniffling, Vivian also hugged Riley. "My hormones have gone haywire. Please don't make me cry!"

While everyone was still laughing at Vivian, Annie pulled Mitch to the side. "Remember Mom's ring?"

His attention still on Riley, Mitch only registered the word ring.

Frowning, he looked down at his sister. "Ring? What ring?"

"Mom's engagement ring, the one she always wore? It's a sapphire with smaller diamonds…"

He nodded, his attention still on the vision in yellow. Damn, she was beautiful. "I remember. What about it?"

"It's yours if you think Riley may like it."

This time, his sister had his attention. "Riley…"

Annie rolled her eyes. "Seriously. You are going to propose tonight, I hope?"

"You mean ask her to marry me?" He shook his head. "There is nothing I would want more than to marry her, but she's been very adamant about the fact she is not interested in ever going down that road again. I'm just happy she wants to be with me."

Sighing, Annie shook her head. "Do yourself a favor and ask her anyway, okay? I'll leave the ring on the table near your front door." And, still shaking her head, she moved toward Craig.

Ring. Married. Riley. Dylan. Everything he hadn't even known he wanted was within his reach. Could he change Riley's mind? Staring at her as she smiled and hugged everyone, he tried to figure out his next move.

Seconds later, he shook his head. He'd never really had time to figure out anything with Riley. Things just happened. And he'd been happy with whatever arrangement she'd wanted. He'd marry her in a heartbeat, but if she just wanted to move in with him, he'd take what he could get. Even if she only stayed for a little while.

After more hugs and good-byes, the family finally left.

Mitch stepped in behind Riley as he waved the family good-bye. As he dropped his hand, he noticed the low back of her dress for the first time. His blood heated instantly as desire punched him in the gut.

With a soft groan, he pulled Riley closer. "Damn, this

dress is driving me crazy." Trailing his hand down her naked flesh, his mouth found her ear. "When can we get out of here?"

She shuddered, leaned against him. "I think someone is going to make a speech at some point; I should probably stay for that. Would you mind?"

"Yes, I mind," he growled. "I can't wait to be alone with you."

Frowning, she turned toward him. "I'm sorry…"

He grinned. "Don't mind me. I'm frustrated. Of course, I'll wait for you; I'm so proud of you. As long as I can be close to you, I'm happy."

Just then, someone tapped on the microphone. Pulling Riley close to him, Mitch put his arms around her. He wasn't quite sure how it had happened, but they'd been given another chance. And he was going to make damn sure he wasn't messing it up this time.

Chapter Nineteen

It took another hour before Riley felt comfortable to leave the exhibition. As she and Mitch left the gallery, her hand still in his, her mind was busy.

Her portraits weren't for sale, much to the disappointment of several clients of the gallery, but the interest in her work had her thinking it was maybe time to get serious about portrait studies. Her first love would always be fashion photography, but if she and Dylan were to move to Marietta...

"Here we are," Mitch said as he unlocked Craig's car and opened the door for her. "When we drove here earlier today, I had no idea I would leave here a much happier man. I'd asked my sisters to help me win you over, but not in my wildest dreams could I have foreseen you'd be here tonight. You've made me a very happy man." Bending down, he kissed her.

The kiss was hot and wet and urgent. By the time he lifted his head, they were both breathing heavily.

"Let's get home," she gasped.

Laughing, he helped her into the car. "I like the sound of

that."

The road wasn't busy, fortunately, and with her hand in Mitch's, the half-hour drive to Marietta flew by.

As they drove into the small town, Riley smiled as she leaned forward. "Every house seems to be decorated for Christmas. It's beautiful."

"People around here are big on Christmas." Mitch smiled. "Annie is in her element—she's always loved Christmas."

"So does Aunt Janice. She came to stay with us when my mom passed away. I'll never forget the first Christmas we had with her. My mom also loved decorating our house, but Aunt Janice takes it to a whole new level. One year she had…"

But they'd reached Mitch's house. As he parked the car, her words faltered, the zoo in her tummy coming alive.

"You okay?" he asked quietly. "If you'd rather I take you back to Janice, just say the word."

"I am exactly where I want to be. Only… I'm not sure if we're on the same page. I think we have to talk…"

With a soft curse, Mitch opened his door. "Let's talk inside."

Biting her lip to prevent it from quivering, she waited for him to open her door. Everything she'd ever wanted was within her reach, but what Mitch didn't know was how loving him had healed her, had changed her heart.

He was miffed. Well, that was too bad. He wasn't always

going to get his way. Lifting her chin, she got out of the car. It was high time Mitch learned that at times she was going to change her mind.

Although his teeth were clenched tightly together, Mitch took her hand as he led her up the pathway to his front door. Without saying a word, he unlocked the door and pushed it open.

Before she realized what he was about to do, he picked her up. "I don't know what page you are on, but I'm on the page of I don't ever want to be without you again. Is that clear?"

Stepping inside the house, he kicked the door closed behind them before he slid her slowly down to the floor. His body was hot, hard, and the expression in his eyes nearly had her falling in a puddle at his feet. But before anything happened, she had a few things on her mind.

Taking off her coat, she stepped back. "I want to be with you, too, but I don't want to move in with you."

He'd already gotten rid of his own coat and dropped both on the closest chair. His eyes were hooded, not giving anything away. "I hauled that damn suitcase all the way to Portland. I told you I'm happy to live with you in your house if that is what you want to do. It doesn't matter where we live, as long as I can be with you."

"That's not what I want."

MITCH'S HEART DROPPED to the ground. What the hell? Clenching his teeth, he counted to ten before he tried to speak.

He was not messing this up again. "Then what the hell do you want, Riley? I told you I love you, and even though you've yet to tell me in so many words how you feel about me, I know you love me, too. I've seen your work tonight."

Lifting her chin, her eyes a fiery blue, she glared at him. "I can't move in with you."

Inhaling deeply, he tried to read her face, but she wasn't giving anything away. There was something else going on here; quite what it was, though, he didn't know.

"So tell me what you want, Riley, because I sure as hell have no idea what to say at this point."

Crossing her arms, she gave him a saucy smile. "You once asked me what it was you have to do so that you can kiss me whenever you want. I've figured it out. What you have to do, Mitch, is marry me."

Speechless, he stared at her. Had she actually said she wanted to marry him or was he hallucinating?

Her smile wavered, and she dropped her arms. "Well, clearly that's not what you had in mind. I... Would you please take me to Aunt Janice?"

Only when her hand reached out to open the front door, did he come out of his stupor. "Where are you going?"

Not looking at him, she opened the door. "It's okay, I'll walk."

Before she could take another step, though, he closed the door, grabbed the small box on the table next to the door he'd noticed as they'd entered, and took Riley's hand. Lacing his fingers with hers, he moved toward the couch in the living room.

Pushing her down on the seat, he crouched in front of her. "You are not going anywhere. I told you I love you; I told you I never want to be without you. I've been waiting for you my whole life. Of course, I damn well want to marry you so that I can kiss you whenever I want to! You were the one who was adamant about not ever marrying again, remember? How the hell was I supposed to know you'd changed your mind?"

She sniffled. "That was before I'd fallen in love with you. Loving you has changed me, healed me. You've changed me. I built high walls around my heart. I never wanted to be hurt again as I was hurt when my parents passed away, and I certainly never wanted to experience the pain and humiliation of being left at the altar." Her eyes were bright with tears. "But then I met you—yelling and punching my brother one moment, crouching down and listening patiently to my son in the next. You've broken down the walls. You've touched my heart because, for some or other reason, you get me. I'm sorry I've sent you away in Portland. You see, I didn't think I was good enough for you, for marriage. But you love me. I'm not easy to live with. When I'm working, I forget about the rest of the world, but I can promise you I'll always love you. And…"

Joy exploded inside his chest, but trying to keep his cool, he kneeled down and opened the box in his hand. "Can you shut up for one moment, damn it? This is my mom's ring. We can find you another one, but Riley O'Sullivan, I love you. I didn't go looking for love, but there you were, red hair, gorgeous blue eyes, and legs that had me drooling, challenging me at every turn, making me rethink what I was saying and how I was reacting and I realized I've always been waiting for you. I want to spend the rest of my life with you. Will you please marry me?"

One lone tear rolled over her check. "I have a son."

Smiling, he wiped the tear away with his thumb. "I actually fell in love with him way before I realized how I feel about you. I can't wait to be his dad and I hope… Maybe you should answer my question first."

With a tremulous smile, she put out her hand. "I've already told you I want to marry you."

With infinite care, he took out the ring. For a moment, he saw his mom clearly, smiling at him, wearing the same ring. Swallowing against the lump in his throat, he slid the ring over Riley's fingers. It seemed to be a perfect fit. "As I've said, we can buy you a new one as soon as the shops open tomorrow…"

Lifting her hand, Riley blinked a few times. "I don't want another ring. I love that it was your mom's ring. I'll wear it with pride. Finish your question—you hope?"

He got up and held out his hand. As he pulled her close to him, the scent of orange blossoms seeped through his pores. "We'll talk more later. But now I want to make love to my fiancée."

⁂

THIS TIME THEY took it slow. Mitch carried her all the way up the stairs, never taking his eyes off of her. In his room, he put her down slowly before he turned her around. "The back of this dress…" Bending down, his hot mouth slid down her back while his fingers found the tiny buttons.

By the time her dress had pooled around her ankles, she was shuddering with need. While Mitch got rid of his clothes, she got onto the bed. Lifting herself on her elbows, she watched him.

Days earlier, she had still been running around, trying to finalize everything for tonight's opening. At the time, she'd had only one thing to hold onto—Mitch loved her. With all her quirks and idiosyncrasies. At the time, she'd had no idea that by the end of tonight she'd be wearing his ring.

Mitch kicked off his pants and was about to join her on the bed when he stopped. "Hang on." Quickly he got his phone out of the pocket of his pants, pressed a few buttons, and the first notes of a song filled the room.

Mimicking the word of the song, he joined her on the bed.

Lifting her arms to gather him close, she laughed. "We have a song!"

"Of course, we have a song." Combing her hair back, those extraordinary eyes scanned her face. "You know, I've thought that it was while dancing with you to this song, I fell for you. But that portrait at the exhibition, the one where I'm staring directly at the camera? You took that one long before we danced. Don't ask me how it happened, but, looking at it tonight, it's so obvious I was already in love with you at that point. I probably fell for you way back in February when you and Craig stayed at the B and B."

Smiling up at him, she pulled his head down. "Told you not everything can be explained by only relying on facts."

With his eyes on her, his hand moved slowly over her shoulder, down her side and up again before it closed around one of her breasts. "Will you tell me again?"

She didn't have to ask what he wanted to know. It was easy to read the uncertainty still lurking in his eyes.

Sliding her fingers in his hair, she brought his mouth closer to hers. "I love you, Mitch Miller. I never thought I'd be given another chance at love until you bellowed yourself into my heart."

"You made fun of me." He grinned.

"You were so angry all the time."

"Looking back, I now realize it was probably mostly frustration. I think I loved you long before I saw you."

Laughing, she traced the outlines of his mouth. "Oooh,

you've got lines—I love it. Do you think we can now stop talking so that I can show my fiancé exactly how much I love him?"

※

MITCH WAS STILL staring into Riley's beautiful eyes when she lifted her body in a surprising move and flipped him over. Before he could catch his breath, she was on top of him and he was lying under her. Her gorgeous hair fell down her milk-white shoulders, those perky breasts tantalizingly close to his mouth. What was a man to do but have a taste?

But she had other plans. "Lie back and enjoy. I've been dreaming about this for a long time." With her eyes on him, she slid down his body before, with a grin, she bent down and put her warm, wet lips against his abdomen. "Love, love your six-pack," she mumbled, making him feel ten feet tall.

Her hands were soft but insistent as they followed her mouth farther and farther down his body, sending his blood way beyond boiling point. By the time she reached his loins, he was ready to explode.

With a groan, he reached down and pulled her up. "If you do that, I won't last," he got out. This time he was the one to change their positions so that she was lying beneath him.

"Kiss me?" Slipping her hand around his head, she pulled him down.

SHE HAD TIME to see the flash in his eyes before their mouths met again. His mouth crushed hers in a searing kiss, his tongue eager as it shot through to dance with hers. Restless hands roamed over her flesh, just not touching her breasts, tormenting them both.

Within minutes, she was tangled around him, trying to get as close to him as humanly possible. His breath was ragged when his mouth finally closed around one breast at the same time his hand found her heat. The climax slammed into her, leaving her shuddering and helplessly calling out his name.

"Beautiful," he whispered as he gave her more, took more until everything else around her faded.

All she was aware of was Mitch—his taste, his smell, his urgent hands, the soft words he murmured in her ear. Blinded by need for him, she took him in her hand, reveled in his low moan as they rolled over the bed.

Finally, Mitch hoisted himself above her, gripped her hands as he entered her, those extraordinary eyes darkened by desire. Trying to keep her eyes on him, she quickly found his rhythm, rode with him until together they reached the peak. His head dropped back, and with a feral growl, he called out her name over and over until, together, they crested.

Chapter Twenty

THEY WERE LATE for breakfast. It was clear by the cars parked in front of Annie's B and B, everyone was still here, waiting for them.

As Mitch opened Riley's door for her, the front door flew open. Annie and Vivian stepped out.

"You're late," Annie called out but before Mitch could respond, Dylan appeared between his aunts.

"Mom, Uncle Mitch!" he yelled and raced down the stairs toward them.

Riley ran forward to pick up her son. "I've missed you." She smiled and kissed him.

"Where have you been?" Dylan asked.

"With Mitch. We... I..." She looked at Mitch.

Mitch stepped closer. "I have something I need to ask you."

"What do you want to ask me?" As Riley put Dylan down, he grabbed one of Mitch's hands.

"Come on, Riley." Vivian smiled. "We're dying to open the bubbly, but it seems we'll have to wait another few minutes."

Annie took one of Riley's arms. "We want to know everything," she said with a wink in Mitch's direction.

Craig and Aiden also stepped out onto the porch, Aunt Janice right behind them.

"What have we missed?" she wanted to know.

Vivian pointed toward Mitch. "Mitch wants to talk to Dylan."

"Oh?" Craig said. "I think Aiden and I should also be a part of that conversation."

Riley groaned. "Seriously, you two…"

Mitch took Dylan's hand. "It's okay, sweetheart, let's all go in. This is a family affair, after all."

Minutes later, they were all sitting around Annie's kitchen table. Craig had opened a bottle of bubbly, and everyone had a glass in front of them. Dylan was sitting on Mitch's knee, looking at everyone with big eyes, sipping on the grape juice Annie had poured him.

"So, Mitch," Aiden said. "I believe you have something to say."

Mitch grinned. "I wanted to talk to Dylan, but okay, since we've moved to Marietta, I've been getting used to sharing just about everything with everyone." He turned to Dylan so that he faced the boy. "Dylan, I want to marry your mom. Would that be okay, do you think?"

Dylan stared at him for a few minutes. Mitch swore he could hear the wheels grinding in the little boy's mind.

"We'll have another wedding?"

Mitch nodded. "That's right."

"So you'll be her husband?"

"I will be her husband."

"She never wanted one before."

Mitch grinned. "I changed her mind. Look, I've even given her a ring."

Riley lifted her hand for Dylan to see.

It was quiet around the table as Dylan chewed on this piece of information.

"Will you have babies?"

Mitch's eyes found Riley's. He hadn't gotten around to discussing the topic with Riley last night. He had no idea whether she'd want another baby.

Touching Mitch's arm, Riley leaned forward. "How would you feel about that?" Riley asked Dylan.

He nodded, his eyes still on Mitch. "I'd like a little brother. When you have a baby, will you be their daddy?"

In that moment, Mitch finally understood what the little boy really wanted to know.

He nodded. "Yes, I'll be their daddy. I could also be your dad. Do you think you would like that?"

His eyes widening, Dylan nodded.

Mitch pulled the little boy close and hugged him. "I'd be honored to be your dad."

The next moment, Dylan jumped to the ground and rushed around the table to where Janice was sitting. "My Christmas m'racle, Aunt Janice."

Janice was openly crying. Sniffling, she wiped her eyes and bent down to kiss Dylan's head. "It's not only your Christmas miracle, sweet boy, it's also mine."

"What Christmas miracle?" Mitch asked, not quite sure what they were talking about.

Aunt Janice smiled tremulously. "Dylan asked Santa if you could be his dad."

Mitch had to swallow a few times before he could speak. Riley's hand found his, and he turned to her. "A Christmas miracle indeed," he said.

Aiden cleared his throat. "You may have Dylan's blessing, but you don't have mine and Craig's yet."

Resignedly, Mitch got up and walked around the table to where Aiden and Craig were sitting. "You just want to crush my hand, don't you?"

Grinning, both men got up. "Hell, yeah. Remember how you treated us?"

Enduring their very hearty handshakes and ribbing, Mitch found Riley's eyes across the table.

Her eyes were bright with tears, but she was smiling. He'd probably always be amazed he'd been given the chance to meet her, to fall in love with her, and to know she loved him, too.

"So, when are you getting married?" Annie asked. "Because I have to warn you, the gossip mill is probably already spreading rumors about Craig's car parked in front of Mitch's house last night. Someone would've seen something."

"When is Christmas?" Mitch asked.

"Monday," Vivian said.

"Riley?" he asked, meeting her eyes. "What about a Christmas wedding?"

"You're crazy!" Annie called out before Riley could open her mouth. "That's the day after tomorrow! The Graff is probably fully booked… except…" Clapping her hands, she stared at Mitch. "How many people do you want to invite?"

"Let's ask my introvert bride." He chuckled.

Riley laughed, and his heart settled. "Just us."

"You sure?" Annie asked. "So we can have it here? On Christmas? We already have a menu; I've made most of the food already. We just need to add more bling. Oh, this is perfect!"

Riley's eyes were bright as she looked at him. "I don't have a dress…"

"Tomorrow," Vivian said. "Craig, Aiden—you two will take Riley to Bozeman to find a dress. Aunt Janice…"

"I'll be here bright and early to help," she said, clapping her hands. "It's perfect, just perfect."

ON CHRISTMAS MORNING, Riley jumped out of bed. Much to Mitch's, and to be quite honest, to her own dismay, Annie had insisted she slept in one of the B and B's beautiful rooms last night.

It was just for one night, though, and she'd enjoyed spending time with Mitch's sisters and Aunt Janice the previous evening.

Aiden and Craig had apparently taken Mitch to a bar. Which one, no one knew. Aunt Janice had warned both her godsons quite a few times to stay away from a place called Wolf Den.

She wouldn't be surprised if that was exactly where her brother and cousin had taken Mitch, but she'd heard when Craig got home last night and it hadn't been that late.

She reached out to pull the curtains aside. Hopefully her bridegroom would be on time…

Her hand froze. Panic reared its head, her heart rate increasing. What if…

Her phone rang. It was a video call from Mitch. With her heart in her throat, she sat down on the closest chair and answered the call. Probably best to be seated. What if he wanted to call the whole thing off?

Mitch's face filled the small screen. Sans shirt, he was smiling at her. "Hi, gorgeous."

Her heart was still beating furiously away. "Why… why are you calling?"

"To tell you I love you and I can't wait for this afternoon when I can make you my wife."

Light-headed from relief, she leaned back against the chair. "Phew, for a moment there, you had me worried."

"What?" Mitch bellowed.

Surprised, she blinked. Mitch was clearly furious. "I..."

But he didn't give her a chance to finish speaking. "I can't believe... Damn it, woman, I love you! Don't you dare move; I'll be with you in two seconds."

As if in a trance, she got up and moved to the window again. Pulling the curtains to the side, she sighed. It was snowing—symbolizing warmth and peace, she'd read somewhere.

Her heart settled. She was marrying Mitch, the man she loved. And of course, he would never...

Her door burst open, a wide-eyed Annie trying to hold onto Mitch's arm. "You're not supposed to see the bride!"

"Damn it, Annie, I need a minute, okay?" And pushing his sister out of the room, he closed the door.

Riley stood frozen on the spot. He'd thrown on a shirt, but it wasn't buttoned up. With long strides, Mitch advanced. His eyes were mere slits, his teeth clenched together.

"I'm sorry," she finally got out as he reached her. Grabbing his hands with hers, she looked up into his eyes. "I panicked. For a moment there... but I know you love me; I know you won't—"

That was as far as she got. Mitch's eyes flashed once before he swooped down and kissed her. She melted against him, her fears finally put to rest.

Lifting his head, he combed her hair out of her eyes. "Are we good?"

Smiling, she slipped her arms around his body, pressing her face against his naked chest. Below her ear, his heart was hammering away. "We're good."

"I have something for you," he said as he reached for his pocket. "I was going to leave it with Annie, but…"

"You can't give me more things…" she began, but ignoring her, he opened a small square box.

With tremulous fingers, she touched the dainty hoop earrings studded with small blue stones all around the circle.

"They're the exact color of your eyes."

Taking them out, she put each one on, never taking her eyes off of Mitch. Mitch dropped the box. Opening his shirt wider, she pressed kisses all over his toned flesh, her hands wandering down to the button of his jeans.

With a laugh, he got rid of his shirt. "Damn it, woman, you'll be the death of me yet." Scooping her up, he walked over to the bed. "I suppose you need more convincing?"

Pulling his head down, she smiled. "Not really, but seeing that you are here…"

He dropped her on the bed. She landed with a small yelp, but before the sound had a chance to echo in the room, his mouth was on hers.

Her arms slid around his neck. It was a good thing the wedding was only this afternoon.

Chapter Twenty-One

MITCH'S HEART HAD still not quite settled by the time he waited for his bride. He should've known Riley might be worried. Hopefully, he'd persuaded her this morning that he'd always show up when he'd promised to. Damn it, he'd been waiting for this moment his whole life.

Annie had turned the huge living room into something out of a fairy tale. Apart from all the Christmas decorations, she'd added more lights, more candles, and dozens of flowers filled every pot she had.

Behind him, the minister was waiting. Craig was standing next to Mitch, making sure he wasn't going anywhere as he'd joked. As if he wanted to be anywhere else than right here. A beaming Janice was sitting in front of them, dressed in shimmering green.

The music began, and as the doors opened, Dylan stepped into the room, holding a small pillow with the rings. Obviously taking his task as ring bearer seriously, his eyes never left the two rings. Sighing audibly with relief as he reached Aunt Janice, he took his seat next to her.

The music changed, and Mitch's heart did a few cartwheels before it settled happily in his chest. His two sisters appeared and walked toward him.

As they took their places, Annie, the closest to him, grabbed his hand for a moment. "So happy for you." Vivian winked at him.

Inhaling deeply, his eyes returned to the door. And there she was. Dressed in layers of flimsy, delicate material, she seemed to float toward him. Her gorgeous red hair fell in loose curls over her milk-white shoulders. He couldn't wait to be with her. With two steps, he'd reached her.

Aiden said something, Mitch nodded, but he didn't really take anything else in except the radiant glow on his bride's face.

"You're here, waiting for me," she said.

"I've always been waiting for you here." He grinned before he bent down and kissed her.

"You s'posed to wait, Dad!" Dylan called out.

Stunned, Mitch looked up. "Just wait here," he told Riley and walked toward Dylan.

※

IT WAS QUIET in the big room as everyone watched Mitch whispering to Dylan. Riley had to swallow a few times at the picture of the big man crouching down in front of her son and Dylan's arm lying trustfully on Mitch's shoulder. The next moment, Mitch stood up and with Dylan's hand in his, they both approached her.

"I'm also getting married to Mitch," Dylan explained as he took her hand.

Riley gave up the struggle to not cry. Tears streamed down her face as Mitch took her other hand.

"He called me Dad," he said softly as he wiped her tears away.

"Mom, you can't cry now. We have to listen to this guy," Dylan whispered loudly.

Laughing through her tears, Riley squeezed Mitch's hand.

She was so glad this guy had waited for her.

BY MIDNIGHT, EVERYONE was sitting around Annie's kitchen table. Mitch had his hand on Riley's shoulder, and he couldn't wait to take her home.

Dylan was fast asleep already and would spend the night at Annie and Craig's. For the next few days, Dylan was going to spend the time between Janice and his sisters while Mitch took Riley to a tropical beach for a few days.

"Aunt Janice." Vivian smiled. "Come on, surely you can tell us now? You've been playing matchmaker all along, haven't you? First with Aiden, then with Craig, and finally with Riley."

Smiling, Janice got up. "Well, as you know, when you're

Irish, matchmaking is a skill you're born with," she said, her Irish lilt more pronounced than usual.

"I knew it." Aiden laughed. "That's why you asked me to visit you. You planned the whole thing from the start."

"But I did no such thing. I was happy here, Marietta is such a wonderful place to live, and I've made such lovely friends here. I've missed you all, though," Janice said. "I was worried about you, too. Aiden, both you and Craig were seeing women you had nothing in common with and Riley was so hurt, she decided she'd never marry again. So, when I met Annie and Vivian and Mitch, we just clicked, and I thought it would be so nice if we could all be friends. But never in my wildest dreams…"

Everyone burst out laughing.

"Yeah, right," Aiden said as he got up and hugged his aunt. "But I will forever be grateful you invited me to write about Marietta and Valentine's Day."

Craig joined them, also putting an arm around Janice. "And I thank you for guilting Annie into using my marketing skills."

Riley also got up. "I still can't believe you faked being ill to get me to visit you so that I'd see Mitch again."

"You completely misunderstood me," Janice said, the picture of innocence. "In any case, by that time, you and Mitch were both already in love with each other."

Mitch found Riley's eyes. "I won't ask you how you knew something I only figured out later, but thank you."

Grabbing his bride's hand, he pulled her close. "Thanks for everything, we're going home. And thanks for taking care of Dylan for a few days."

MITCH CARRIED HER up the stairs. "We have so much to talk about, but it can all wait until we're back. I have one more surprise for you, though."

Her head resting against her husband's wide chest, Riley smiled. "I don't think I can handle any more surprises. You've already given me so much."

At the top of the stairs, he put her down and took her hand. "It's just to show how happy I am you've agreed to be my wife, agreed to change your whole life to be with me."

He turned away from the side of the house where his bedroom was. "We can change anything you want, but I hope you can make this your office, studio, workplace—whatever you want to call it." Opening the door to one of the other rooms upstairs, he switched on the light.

She stepped into the room. "Oh, Mitch," she cried, looking at the freshly painted walls, the desk, the bookcase, the new curtains. "It's perfect. I've never had a separate room I could work in. When did you do all this?"

He pulled her close. "Turns out, the townsfolk of Marietta are very happy to welcome another photographer into their midst. Everyone in town pitched in to help. And now,

I'm taking you to our bed." Picking her up, he walked toward his room. "I know you must be tired, so have a bath and sleep…"

Pulling his head down, she stopped his words. There were things her husband still had to learn about her. Such as the fact that, never mind how tired she was, when he touched her, she was ready for him.

Hours later, she got up and opened the curtains. It was still snowing softly. Hugging herself, she smiled. Warmth and peace. Her heart had finally settled. She'd found her home where a heart had been waiting for her—in Marietta.

The End

If you enjoyed *Merry Christmas, Montana*,
you'll love the next book in…

The Millers of Marietta series

Book 1: *My Montana Valentine*

Book 2: *A Match Made in Montana*

Book 3: *Merry Christmas, Montana*

Available now at your favorite online retailer!

More Books by Elsa Winckler

The Cavallo Brothers series

Book 1: *An Impossible Attraction*

Book 2: *An Irresistible Temptation*

Book 3: *The Ultimate Surrender*

Available now at your favorite online retailer!

About the Author

I have been reading love stories for as long as I can remember and when I 'met' the classic authors like Jane Austen, Elizabeth Gaskell, Henry James The Brontë sisters, etc. during my Honours studies, I was hooked for life.

I married my college boyfriend and soul mate and after 43 years, 3 interesting and wonderful children and 3 beautiful grandchildren, he still makes me weak in the knees. We are fortunate to live in the picturesque little seaside village of Betty's Bay, South Africa with the ocean a block away and a beautiful mountain right behind us. And although life so far has not always been an easy ride, it has always been an exciting and interesting one!

I like the heroines in my stories to be beautiful, feisty, independent and headstrong. And the heroes must be strong but possess a generous amount of sensitivity. They are of course, also gorgeous! My stories typically incorporate the family background of the characters to better understand where they come from and who they are when we meet them in the story.

Thank you for reading

Merry Christmas, Montana

If you enjoyed this book, you can find more from all our great authors at TulePublishing.com, or from your favorite online retailer.

Made in United States
North Haven, CT
17 July 2025